The Heroes of
The Elemental Academies

Dragon's Breath

Stratford Ukena

ISBN 978-1-957582-06-1 (paperback)
ISBN 978-1-957582-07-8 (eBook)

Printed in the United States of America

Chapter 1: Fire in the Night

Explosions. Explosions are what Seth heard when he was violently pulled from the dream world into the world of the living. At first all Seth could do was stare up at his ceiling and wonder why he had awoken before the sun. The answer wasn't long in coming, another explosion shook the entire foundation of his home in the Lightforce Academy. dust fell from the rafters of his house making him sneeze violently as he threw his covers back and leapt out of bed. Seth didn't understand what was going on at the moment, but one thing was clear, the Academy was under attack. Seth ran to his closet, smacking his knee on his bed frame. Resisting the urge to curse as he grabbed his knee in pain Seth continued to hobble to his closet which lay at the foot of his bed.

Another explosion turned night into day outside his window and the resounding impact bore into his skull with the force of a thunderclap. Seth shook it off and grabbed the handle of the wooden door that lead to his closet. Throwing it open Seth grabbed Sonfang from where it rested inside.

Seth ran his hand lightly over the handle fingering the dark blue gem that was now encrusted in it; The Water Gem. It had planted itself inside his sword after he used it to end the invasion. It had been a year since the demons' invasion. During that time there had been no more demon sightings. And while that was unusual it hadn't been unwelcome. So why the sudden attack out of nowhere.

These thoughts were swirling through Seth's mind as he willed armor made from the light to form around him. Two more explosions rocked the earth outside his window. Seth strapped Sonfang's scabbard to his side and bolted for the door his heavy armored boots causing the wood to creak as he ran.

Throwing open the door to his house Seth was greeted by a terrible sight. The city of the Lightforce Academy was in flames. People, agents and civilians both were sprawled in the streets. The agents were attempting to protect the civilians from the threat that seemed to be originating from the sky. In front of Seth a man standing protectively over two children roared at the sky. Looking up Seth saw the threat for the first time. Seth swallowed hard. As a thread of fear crawled its way into his heart. His mind just simply couldn't believe what he was seeing in front of him. A black dragon cloaked in darkness descended upon them. Opening its maw and belching a black fire down toward Seth. Seth knew he should move but at that moment his entire body froze. The fire engulfed him in a swirling blaze that inflicted upon him more pain than he could've imagined. Seth couldn't help it he screamed it and screamed, the feeling of his flesh melting and blood boiling driving him to madness. His vision began to go dark until finally all he knew was blackness.

Suddenly a scream tore from his mouth and he bolted upright. It was then that he knew that he was still in bed. That everything that had just happened had been a dream. Seth was drenched in sweat and his breathing was erratic. But he noticed none of that. One thought filled his mind as he began taking deep breaths to calm himself. Something was coming, something big and he had to warn the Academy.

Struggling, he got out of bed and donned his armor. Grabbing Sonfang he walked briskly out of his room. He knew just who to talk to. Hopefully he was still up. He left his house in the middle of the night in search of the one person who would know what to do. He went to find Strat Bannot.

Chapter 2: A Hit and Run

Stratos Bannot

Strat Bannot, protector of the Academy was asleep in his king-sized bed, wrapped in his soft Egyptian cotton sheets the last thing he wanted to do was get out of bed. So, when a urgent knock on his door disrupted his slumber you can be sure he was remiss to answer it. But then another knock came and another.

Struggling out of bed was about as bad as fighting a demon king. Whoever it was, was about to get an earful. Stumbling, he made his way down the hallway toward his front door passing by the hallway pictures that depicted his many friends over the long, long years. He paid them no mind. One of the only things Strat had to look forward to over the Many years he'd been alive was when he was able to sleep. So, when someone woke him...

Another knock on his door sounding more like a desperate bang this time. "I'm coming you lout!" Strat exclaimed angrily. Reaching the door Stray threw it open expecting to see Seth, who had woken him up several nights before to tell him about a dream of dragons attacking g the Academy. But instead a lonely agent stood on his front porch, looking very wet and very tired. Which wasn't surprising seeing as it was raining. The sweet musky smell of rain on grass permeated the air. But the agent looked as if he'd ran here in a very big hurry.

In fact, Strat realized that this particular agent was one of the ones he'd sent out on patrol to keep a look out for enemies approaching from the sky.

Strat woke quickly adrenaline pushing his drowsiness from his body like white cells do infections.

"What is it private Helio?" Strat asked his tone severe. The private took a moment to collect himself before looking up at him.

"Sir Malcovitch was right they are coming."

"How long till they get here." Strat had already summoned his armor and was preparing to raise the alarm but he never got the chance because just then explosion rocked the market square lighting up the night. The ground rumbled and shook the entire academy.

"Sir they are already here," Helio replied. Strat sighed in annoyance, it looked as if he wouldn't be going back to sleep anytime soon.

"Raise the alarm I need you to be ready for anything." Strat order then he willed his double-sided trident to his side. It was time to go to work.

Seth Malcovitch

When the explosion erupted in the market Seth wasn't surprised in the least. In fact, he was already ready for combat. For the last week since his dream Seth hadn't been able to sleep. Well not well anyway. He had been keeping watch over the main northern wall with the other agents on duty. Although they had asked him to rest he just couldn't bring himself to do it. So, when the explosion hit Seth had been waiting for it. And just like his dream the dark shadows of seven enormous flying lizards blocked out the stars. Seth drew Sonfang as one of the dark shadows neared his position on the wall. Seth willed wings of light to appear on his back and took flight. Pushing towards the ground with his wings Seth ascended to block the path of the behemoths. The behemoths responded to immediately breaking up and scattering in different directions to attempt to go around him.

Seth had been tormented with the dreams of these dragons for a week so he wasn't fazed by seeing them in person. The dark webbed wings trailing a cloud of darkness that seemed to be trying to drain the light of his wings. The glowing red eyes shrouded in black fire did little to unsettle Seth. The body of the dragon was as wide as a school bus and as long as two of them.

Covered in hardened black scales that managed an ethereal glow. Only one dragon had stayed put to face Seth probably to keep him from going after the other dragons. This didn't bode well for it meant this had been planned. Seth raised Sonfang and prepared to fight.

The dragon made the first strike. With surprising speed, the dragon spun on a dime lashing out with his spiked tail. Seth threw up his weapon in defense while also adding a defense Light barrier sphere around him. Seth had been training nonstop with Strat and Jack since they had saved the Academy. However, the strength of a mythical creature couldn't be taken for granted. Seth managed to block it but he was sent flying to the ground. Seth smashed into a tavern roof and barreled straight through to the first floor. The resulting crater that was left was by no means small. Seth's light barrier protected him but that didn't mean it didn't hurt. Coughing Seth struggled to his feet. His breathing was ragged and strained. He looked up to the roof of the tavern.

One of Seth's wings had been injured when he fell but Seth simply repaired it with the light. Seth had been waiting for this attack for a whole week. He wasn't about to be taken out of the fight so easily. Seth crouched and raised his wing in the air.

Jumping as high as he could Seth flapped his wings and shot up through the top of the tavern ready to battle the dark dragon. Only to find that it was gone. Quickly Seth spun around in search of the beasts... But they had all left. The only sounds were the crackling of fires that had spread across the city, and the panicked cries of the Academies' citizens.

Chapter 3: These Lively Days

Stratos Bannot

The clean-up effort from the previous night's attack had been long underway when Strat was finally able to get out of the emergency war council Samson had called. Strat hadn't deigned to inform Samson of Seth's dream so Samson had been a little agitated but soon calmed down after Strat explained his reasons. Because they had had no idea if Seth's dream had been a warning of just a dream they refrained from telling anyone to avoid worrying everyone for nothing. Counter measures were put into place to avoid surprise attacks like that again. But Strat knew it was still far from over. The attack last night was done for a reason. It wasn't a random attack like most of the council thought. Unless their enemy was a fool. (Which Strat could assure them, he isn't.) Then an attack and then retreat could only mean the enemy was attempting to distract the Academies

forces from their true objective.

As to what that could be Strat had no idea. The obvious path

would be to sneak a small team of elite demons inside the Academy

under the cover of the attack. But after reviewing the defenses, the

were able to conclude that this was not the case. However, that didn't

leave them with many options. Another possibility is assassination but

guards were already posted outside the houses of the commander's

and even a few inside. (Which Strat found extremely annoying. No

one had managed to assassinate him in two thousand years. Not for

lack of trying. But Samson insisted, so what can you do.)

As Strat was walking down the still rubble strewn street he

caught a glimpse of Seth up ahead in the market square. Being the

first place to be hit it had the most damage done to it. Strat watched

as Seth utilized his abilities over water to put out remaining fires and

to sweep away debris.

At the same time Seth was restoring the building with his

use of both nature and earth elements. Strat was really impressed

with Seth's growth. Not six months before Seth could only use one element at a time. But now that he'd been working so diligently he was improving by leaps and bounds. Strat approached Seth as he was coordinating with some earthen agents who were part of the reconstruction team.

"If we put a new line of houses there then that would buy us enough time to..." The agent paused as Strat approached. This was something that always managed to annoy Strat. Whenever he was around everyone seemed to be unable to work around him. It made him uncomfortable to think that he couldn't just be in an area for fear of nothing getting done.

"Oh Lord Bannot, what a pleasant surprise," said the earthen agents while making a short bow. This agent looked to be in his late twenties or early thirties, with rough salt and pepper hair. He wore a weathered face whose scars foretold the many battles he'd no doubt been in.

"So, how's the reconstruction progressing?" Strat asked out of curiosity.

"It going well, very well sir."

"Good I love to hear it."

"If you don't mind I'm going to borrow Lord Malcovitch for a moment."

The agents nodded. "Of course, Lord Bannot. But if you would excuse us we have more work to do." Strat said nothing as he watched the agents move away discussing rebuilding plans as they went.

"So, what did you need to speak to me about?" Seth asked eyeing Strat carefully.

"Oh, nothing much," Strat shrugged wanting nothing more than to be home in bed resting right about now.

"I just wanted to inform you of the things discussed in the counsel since you couldn't be there."

"Oh?" Seth's voice went serious.

"Yeah Samson was a little irritated at first that we hadn't let him know about your dream. But when I explained why we had kept it a secret he seemed to calm down." Strat studied Seth curiously. It wasn't common for someone, even in the Academies to have prophetic dreams. So, the fact that Seth had one was troubling to say the least. The only ones that were known to have prophetic dreams were the elves. But Seth had nothing to do with them so the fact that he had them was troubling to say the least.

"Did they figure out how the barrier was by passed," Seth asked. At this question Strat knew his eyes had gone cold because he felt Seth shiver then start release a warm aura to defend against the waves of cold coming of Strat.

"Yeah we figured it out and it seems pretty likely."

"What does?" Seth asked his nervousness at what Strat was going to reveal was palpable.

"Good, you should be nervous," Strat thought. "Because what I'm going to tell you is very alarming."

"Well what is it?" Seth asked again impatiently.

Strat lowered his voice to a whisper and beckoned Seth to lean in. It was then Strat spoke the word he never thought he'd ever utter again. "We have a traitor here in the Academy!"

Chapter 4: Recovery

Seth Malcovitch

"Traitors!" Seth exclaimed. "How do you mean?" Seth saw Strat sigh.

"I mean exactly what I said. I mean people who reject what God's done for them and would instead rather side with the devil." Seth could feel an unsettling tightness in his chest. It was a feeling of uncertainty at the idea of these people that Seth would never understand.

"I know you didn't even know that it was possible for the Lightforce to have any Traitors but in truth we are human just like anyone else. Seth followed Strat a few more paces as they continued to walk.

"So, how are the repairs coming.?" Strat asked. Seth didn't even hear him. He was so focused on the thoughts running through his head that he didn't even acknowledge that Strat had spoken. He was more worried about who he could trust. Because he didn't want to inadvertently screw over the Academies based on something he said while thinking he was among friends. The thought was so foreign not too long ago he had had trouble believing what was going on around him. In fact, he had called King Samson out on it and denied what was happening. In doing so he'd denied the many deaths that had also happened, as well as the validity of the Lightforce's beliefs. This had led to all sorts of conflicts between him and his new comrades.

Now to find out that there were people who God had helped that were doing exactly that made Seth wonder if he hadn't come to believe just what would have become of him. Would he have ended up just like these people who had rejected God's help and love, or would he have taken a darker path.

Fortunately, his thoughts were interrupted by Strat who took that moment lightly punch Seth's shoulder probably to jostle him out of his thoughts. Except Strat's idea of a light tap felt like a heavy weight fighter hit him in his arm, nearly knocking him over. Seth stumbled, trying to regain his balance for he toppled over and made a fool of himself.

"What was that for!?" He exclaimed glaring accusingly at Strat. But Strat just laughed and shook his head.

"Sorry, I didn't think I hit you that hard," he said with a smirk. Seth who was still irritated did not laugh. Strat put his hand up as if to compel Seth to calm down. "Look, I'm sorry, but I don't think it will do anybody good if we think too much on this. The last thing we need is to be at each other's throats" Seth sighed knowing that Strat was right. Strat put a hand on Seth's shoulder. "Come on I'll treat you to some breakfast."

"Breakfast? Where?" Seth inquired as he followed Strat who began walking deeper into the Academy

"How about at the Dragon's Rest," Strat suggested thoughtfully. "You know the inn that sells hamburgers now."

"Is it even still standing?"

"It better be. Because right now i'm in sore need of a cup of coffee, and if i don't get it todays going to be unpleasant for everyone near me." Seth had witnessed Strat without his coffee and it was a truly terrifying sight. Arguably one of the most powerful people in the academy, and the first thing he was worried about after an enemy attack was whether or not the coffee and hamburger place made it.

They made their way down the street they were on, heading in the general direction of the Inn in question. It was perhaps a thirty-minute walk but it felt much longer than that with all the bustle and movement of all the academy agents hard at work. There was too much to do. It didn't help that according to the reports coming in the dragons, hadn't left the academy lands, in fact they were seen circling the sky only about 30 miles away from the northern gate, which had led them to believe a second attack was probably imminent.

But a few side streets that they passed actually seemed worse than the others. There were still quite a few fires burning filling the air with a smoky haze. Tears threatened to flood Seth's eyes as the smoke hit him. Seth simply lowered his head and kept going forward following Strat who seemed to walk unfazed through acidic smoke.

After another five minutes of walking Strat and Seth emerged from the smoke cloud right in front of Talon street. This street held a lot of the Academies' lodgings as well as a few renowned restaurants.

It was a tourist spot for people coming into the Lightforce city for the first time. However now, it looked like a warzone. The whole street had been effectively decimated. The cobbles were blackened with fire and the heat that radiated from them could be felt even from several paces away.

The building along both sides of the street had been reduced to rubble. Where once they had stood tall welcoming visitors with warmth and food they were now empty burning husks. The sight saddened Seth, so much so that his eyes threatened to well up again, but this time it wasn't because of the smoke. But instead of crying Seth reached into himself to find the power he'd been gifted. As he did he felt the overwhelming power of the Water Gem flow into him.

At first Seth was afraid the power would overtake him but refocusing his mind and putting his faith in the fact that if God had given him this power, then he would be sure Seth could and would use the power for his kingdom. Seth imagined a flowing river within him and guided the flow of energy to match the picture. And instead of trying to force the power to bend to his will he decided to cut away at the bank and make new paths for the power to travel through. This effectively allowed Seth to control the flow of the power he'd been given.

After channeling the power through his body to the palm of his upraised hand, he formed a picture in his mind. He pictured the rain falling from the sky with enough force to quench the fires within the area but nothing more. It was only after very clearly picturing it that he was able to them release the power from his hand into the world around him.

Seth opened his eyes to find nothing had changed. At first a bolt of panic laced its way through him. If the power didn't do what he'd asked, then what had happened to it. A moment later though a singular droplet of water fell from the sky. It struck his neck and Seth shivered in response to its cool touch. Then after the first a second, and then third, then fourth. Until finally it was pouring rain enough rain that the street went from scorching hot to harboring deceptively deep puddles of water. Seth looked up into the sky only to see that there weren't any clouds. The sun still shined from above.

Seth heard Strat clear his throat and he turned to face him.

"Well so much for a Hamburger," Strat complained as he began to walk down the now steam covered street,

As Strat walked down the street he bumped into a man wearing a long black coat with a hood, he looked back to see who it was, but he was already gone.

Chapter 5: Old Friend

Katie Malcovitch

As Katie approached the small humble abode on edge of the city. She remembered the first time she had ever approached this house. Built into the side of a hill with a cobblestone chimney rising from the stone roof of the building, it was a small building but it was well lived in. Dark black smoke rose from the chinmey signaling that the forge was lit. Katie looked up at the sun and realized it was just passed midday which meant "he" would be taking his lunch break soon.

"Good," she thought she'd hate to interrupt his work. Mostly because she knew that above anything else, he hated interruptions, but partly because what he did was important to the welfare of the Academy as a whole. As she approached, she managed to steel herself against the welcome she was sure to receive. She knocked three times and waited for someone to answer. But as one minute turned to five and nobody came to the door she knocked again. But once more there was no answer. So, she prepared to knock again, but the door was pulled open abruptly and a small heavy set man with a rather large beard.

"Hi Barbrotos," Katie began, but she was soon cut off by thick arm wrapping around her waist and lifting her up.

"Katie! By the Lord you are back!!"

Katie found herself smiling in spite of herself.

"Yes, Barbrotos I've actually been back for almost a year now."

"And it took you this long to come and see your oldest companion?" Katie looked down a little ashamed.

"Well, you could always leave that shack and come out once and awhile," she replied.

"As stubborn as always I see. So, what brings you out to my "shack" as you put it." Katie motioned towards the open door of Barbrotos' house.

"May I?" She asked. His heavily lined eyes widened a bit and he moved toward the house waving for her to follow.

"Come on in. Sorry for the bad manners I don't normally have visitors.

As Katie entered the house, she saw it was a mess. Tools and hammers laid strewn about and the only light in the entire place came from the central fireplace.

"I can see that." Katie studied her old friend happy to see he was in good health. And other than a few grey hairs in his abnormally long beard he looked no different. Katie sat down at the table which besides a low cot, a few chairs, and an old shabby looking stool, was the only furniture that seemed to be in the house. Barbrotos sat down across from her after pouring them both glasses of water. Katie took a sip before setting it down.

"How old are you now?" She asked. Barbrotos raised an eyebrow at her.

"Asking people's ages, now are we? A bit rude don't you think?" Katie said nothing to that and remained fixed on his face. Soon the smile disappeared from his face and it was replaced by a serious expression. "546, years old this August," he finally replied. Katie sat forward studying his face.

"And you're still healthy? No problems?" She asked.

"No, none. Why are you asking?"

You know why," Katie replied.

"I told you I'm half dwarf they have really long lives, I..."

"They don't live this long. I know I just got back but you know I've been worried about you since..."

"Enough!" Barbrotos thundered stopping their conversation in its tracks.

"The first time you see me in 82 years, and this is what you want to talk about?"

Katie hesitated, "Well no, this isn't why I came I just wanted to make sure you..."

"Then why did you come?" Barbrotos said clearly wanting to change the subject. Katie decided to let it go.

"I'm here for a job request," she said. Her tone adopting a more commanding demeanor. "One only you can do."

His Demeanor changed as well; he became more business-like. Sitting straighter and studying her face intently.

"So, you came here with a job, that is far more likely." He paused. "Well, what are you waiting for what is it?" Katie reached into her pocket and pulled from it a folded piece of paper. She held it across the table to Barbratoss, who promptly took it. He unfolded the paper and looked at its contents. After a few minutes of intently studying the paper he looked at her with wonder on his. face.

"Who came up with this?" He asked, his eyes roaming the page.

"You won't believe this, but it was my son." Amusement entered his expression.

"So basically, he's different from you in that he actually plans his battles." Katie raised an eyebrow before continuing.

"We have to get these made before tomorrow do you think we can do it?"

Barbratoss looked down at the paper in front of him. Katie studied him trying to judge his answer. When his answer did come it was the expected one. Barbratoss squared his shoulders and looked up at her determination in his eyes.

"Well, it doesn't matter if we can or not. I have a reputation to protect so... We will get them done.

Chapter 6: Training

The sun was high in the sky as Seth approached the Colosseum. Seth had only been in a few parts of the gigantic building that towered over all others in the academy. It had One big arena at its center for spectacles and other Academy wide events but also over a hundred smaller arenas surrounded it. These arenas were arranged in a spiral that led to the center grand arena. The further inside you went the smaller the arenas.

It was a good place to get lost. Even with the rooms labeled with letters and number like 2A or 38A all the way to the center at 100A. Even with this measure it was still quite easy to get lost. That is why it was advised within the Academy to never go in the Colosseum alone. As Seth got ever closer to the west entrance the evening training group was getting out. As Seth looked closer at the armor, they were wearing he noticed that they belonged to the 63rd battle group. The group that had been assigned to the west wall along with the 10th battle group. They were among the largest of the battle groups. Usually, agents worked alone or in pairs. Only in times of war where they assigned a battle group and a rank.

As Seth passed them some took notice and nodded in his direction. Seth noticed Strat leaning against the wall by the door wearing a simple chainmail shirt that fit tightly over his normal attire. His back leaned against the wall, he seemed to be watching Seth approach with something like stern interest. His look almost made Seth balk. He wore an expression of excitement. Excitement was not an expression Strat wore often. Seth reached him and stood awkwardly waiting for Strat to speak.

"Alright!" Strat said rubbing his hands together as if he was trying to warm them. "We'll start by teaching you how to navigate using the earth. I'm going to go inside and wait at one of the arenas. Your job will be to locate me using the earth." Seth crossed his arms and gave Strat a look of annoyance.

"That's all really interesting but you forgot one tiny detail."

Strat raised an eyebrow," Oh and what is that."

"Oh, I don't know maybe the fact that you haven't exactly explained how i do that."

"Right, well yeah I should probably do that." Seth smirked.

"I can already see how wise you are," he said.

"Well anyway try closing your eyes."

Seth did as he was instructed. "Now I want you to try to feel the ground through the soles of your feet. Try to imagine the power of earth as an energy in your body sturdy and immovable. Can you do it?" Seth tried to form an image in his mind of a formless substance in his body that moved through out it like the blood in his veins. I took him a few moments to keep the picture firmly in his mind but once he did it became much easier to maintain. It was only after managing that, that he began to feel something in his heels.

Like a warmth that spread from a place just to the right of his heart four energies spread throughout his body. Each one felt different than the others. But only one was what he was looking for. Sturdy and immobile, that was the one he was looking for. After examining each one he finally found the one he was looking for. He grabbed a hold of it and forced it down through the soles of his feet.

But when it left his feet he was able to extend it past his limbs and into the ground. It expanded like a sonic wave through the ground using himself as an epicenter. The first thing it came in contact with was the soles of Strat's boots. It mapped out his entire body and then left. Next came the buildings, Seth was able to map out the entirety of several buildings before he felt Strat tugging at his sleeve.

"Seth, Stop!" Strat exclaimed grabbing him and tugging him off balance. The movement shattered Seth's concentration and the power faded. Seth whipped around pushing Strat off of him.

"What was that for I almost had it!" Strat crossed his arms as if he was dealing with a kid.

"Yeah, I could see that. But you know what, I don't think the residents, most of who are earth elementals that live in this area particularly appreciate their privacy being invaded." Strat nodded behind Seth and Seth turned to see several people some in Lightforce uniforms others in just civilian clothes eyeing Strat and Seth with scowls. Their looks reminded Seth of the same one his mom gave him when he got suspended from one of his schools, intense. Seth felt his cheeks redden as he realized some of the rooms, he had been mapping out had some rather inappropriate things being done.

"It is one of the rudest things you can do," Strat was saying.

"What is?"

"To scan someone before meeting them. It is just one of the customs all earth elementals abide by." Strat waved to the people who were now watching them, and they seemed to relax going back to their day-to-day activities.

"Now, you can use this in the Colosseum but don't extend past its boundaries. So, shall we begin." "I'll go into the Colosseum and then you will wait twenty minutes and then try to follow. got it?"

Seth nodded an affirmative still trying to shake what he seen in the rooms out of his head.

"Yeah, I got it," he replied.

After Strat had gone in Seth stood outside waiting. Since he did not have a way to tell exactly Seth waited till, he was sure twenty minutes had passed and then he entered as well going straight for the center, his feet clicking against the stone floor. Seth pictured the energies in his head again drawing upon the abilities god had given him. As he once extended energy out from the souls of his feet in a shockwave, he managed to locate Strat easily. He wasted no time getting there either. As he entered the training arena Strat began to clap.

"Well done! You catch on well. But now its time to learn how to direct the earth, to actually bend it to your will."

The arena they were in like all the other arenas was circular but this one was also split into four sections. Each section was dedicated to a different element. The one Strat was standing in was the earth element. The floor was made of many different kinds of stone. Quartz, marble, obsidian, cobblestone, limestone, even Flint was present in some amount.

Seth walked over to where Strat was waiting.

"Today I'm going to teach you fluidity. You must learn to adapt the way you think about the earth. About stone in general. Stone is sturdy, rigid and strong, but it is also soft life giving and at times even fluid." Seth's confusion was obvious, and Strat put his hand on his head releasing a sigh of exasperation.

"I guess it was too much to expect you to understand with just words.

"Sorry," Seth said. Seth was more of a visual learner.

"Alright I want you to stand over there," Strat said pointing to a spot near the middle of the training room. Seth complied unsure of where this was going. "Okay I'm going to throw several attacks at you the normal way and we'll have you block them."

Seth nodded his understanding his mind already reaching for the power he knew was there. After a Curt not between the both of them to ensure they were both ready Strat launched the first attack.

He stomped the earth and the ground spat out four rectangular boxes of pure stone. Strat then swept his left and right arms out in a punching gesture. Seth didn't wait to see what Strat was going to do because he had a pretty good idea of how he was going to attack him. Seth raised his arms in a defensive x and the ground raised in a wall of earth five feet tall and at least that big across.

Seth felt the wall shake as the blocks impacted the wall. After a few minutes Seth imagined the wall lowering back into the earth and it obliged.

"Good! Good!" Strat said. "That was a nice and solid defensive wall. Now, let's do that again and we'll see if you are able to defend against it so easily this time." Seth took a defensive position again. Strat wasted no time this time attacking immediately. A continuous column of earth shot out of the ground straight at Seth. Seth raised another earth shield almost automatically and waited to feel the resounding impact of the column hitting his wall.

Suddenly Seth saw a flash out of the corner of his eye, but he was too late. And impact picked him up off the ground and flung him into the wall of the training arena. Panting Seth immediately recovered.

"What the heck," Seth said trying to see who had attacked him. But he was astonished by what he saw. The column that had shot out of the ground at Strat's feet had stopped inches from his wall and them went out to the right curved around his wall and struck him in the side.

Strat walked up to him and offered a hand. "Do you get what I was talking about now?" He asked helping Seth to his feet. Seth nodded.

"I think so but I'm going to need a lot of practice."

"Good at least you know your own limits," Strat said with a warmness to his voice Seth had rarely heard. Was that pride. Seth stood up.

"We'll we have the entire evening to work so are you willing to work with me?" Strat just nodded. "Well then let's get to work," Seth said with a smile.

Chapter 7: Of Fire and Dragons

As the sun was setting over the western horizon, the city of the Lightforce showed no signs of decreased activity. The civilians were being directed to domed shelters made of conoroid, the strongest metal known to the Lightforce. These domed shelters were placed throughout the Academy and were equipped with the provisions and supplies needed to sustain everyone during a siege. Agents rushed to and from the city wall preparing for the battle to come. Large basins of water were placed throughout the city and teams of water elementists we're on standby to fight fires when necessary. Medical stations were also being setup throughout the city. And agents specializing in air defense guarded them. The city was on high alert. Unlike the last attack the city now had time to prepare. Agents stood in neat rows facing the northern horizon in full armor. Most of the Academy forces were actually deployed on missions to the normal world and thus the Academy was facing this threat with one-third it's total strength.

Seth exited his house battle ready, his armor clinking as he moved, his sword on the side. He walked through the streets towards headquarters where the wall assignments were to be given out. He passed by many agents a mixture of fear and courage on their faces. This wasn't just another day. Fighting armies, saving people, risking their lives, these were things that agents were used to. But dragons... That's a whole new level of danger. Seth arrived outside the HQ to find Strat waiting for him. The familiar sight of Strat's steel and leather armor pulled tight over him put Seth to ease. Strat looked at Seth as he walked up in his armor. Strat raised an appraising eye to Seth.

"Yes Strat, I did put my armor on and did it right at that. So, you can stop staring." Seth hated wearing the armor, he felt silly wearing armor in the twenty first century, so he rarely wore it.

"Not quite right," Strat said as he walked over to Seth and tightened the straps directly under his arms where Seth couldn't really reach. "That is why you should always get someone to help you take your armor off and on."

"Oh, so I missed two little straps, sue me," Seth replied as he joined Strat on the hill overlooking the academy as the sun descended in the west casting the academy in a reddish light that was quickly turning purple.

"It's hard to believe that two years ago I was worried about a math test," Seth said humorously. Strat smiled.

"If there's one thing I've learned in the past two Millenia it's that: you never know what life will throw at you." He paused. "Well, it's me and you on the north wall," Strat said. "Not that I expected anything else. You have the water gem, and I am the protector so that makes us the best choices for it. Since we are balanced in offense and defense. They need Jack to guard the East wall and your mom's taking the west wall, the south wall is being guarded by the elites. So, we will be in the north. We will be commanding well over 2000 men; do you think you are up for that?"

"Do you want me to be honest?" Seth responded suddenly finding it hard to swallow.

"Well, they do say that honesty is the best policy."

"Then, no I don't think I'm ready at all. This is my first large scale battle not to mention it's a siege, how could I possibly know how to lead these guys?" Strat nodded as if he had expected Seth to say as much.

"Well then just focus on fighting and staying alive, I'll do the commanding.

Remember this is a first for a lot of us. Dragons don't usually attack settlements they much rather prefer to stay neutral, so I expect that after this battle, assuming we survive. We will be also sent on a mission to find out whatever is causing this breach in neutrality, as well as to find out their goal."

Seth nodded, "figures. Well, we better get into position."

"Yeah, you're right." As Seth followed Strat down the hill towards the city, he hardened his heart for the battle to come.

The sun had now been down for almost thirty minutes and a nervous calm had settled over the city. Seth stood atop the northern walls behind the bulwark of white stone, behind him nearly two thousand men and women some young, others in their middle ages but they all wore determined looks on their faces. Shoulder to shoulder they stood. Here differences in size, sex, age, or race didn't matter for they were all children of God and they were all in it together.

Not thirty minutes ago, a rider had ridden in to inform Strat that the dragons were on their way. Only about thirty miles out. Which was equivalent to two minutes by air. This was it. Seth took a deep breath and drew his sword, Sonfang from its scabbard. The rest of the agents behind him did likewise drawing their weapons to prepare for the fight ahead.

It wasn't long in coming. The first thing they heard was the loud multitude of thunderous roars that shook the entire land. They were definitely coming. An order was given and up and down the walls flood lights about fifteen feet across and spread out on the wall every thirty feet, were turned on and pointed up at the sky. The giant new machines were also loaded. These machines were giant ballistae that shot massive heat sinking bolts at the enemy.

But there were only five of them spread throughout the wall even Barbratoss couldn't have completed any more Seth was just happy that he had gotten that many done. A final horn rang signaling that the dragons would soon be within sight. And then the dragons were there, they didn't slowly come into sight like Seth thought they were going to, no they just popped up like a science fiction film with ships dropping out of hyperspace. It was instantaneous. The first thing Seth noticed was that there must have been Almost two dozen of them ranging from all shapes and sizes. Some had talons lining their backs others had overly long horns but all of them were still menacing.

The next thing Seth noticed was the black fire as it belched from their mouths. At least forty feet it raged outwards scouring across the wall. Seth saw many light shields burst into being but several quickly burned out. Screams drowned the night in sound as battle was commenced. Light bolts, fire bolt and even some lightning few from the walls lashing out at the dragons. The dragons split, each spreading out and easily avoiding the attack as they continued their approach towards the walls. They fought like fighter jets making a bombing run as they swept low over the walls spitting fire and swiping with their talons. Seth realized that there was one heading in his direction of the wall. Seth imagined a giant gilded spear of light almost thirty feet in length appearing in the air in front of the wall and a brilliant flash of light lit up the wall causing the dragon to roar in protest and attempt to veer out of the way. Seth launched the spear at him willing it through the air with amazing speed however the spear only managed to graze the dragon Seth was aiming for, but it struck the one behind it directly in the chest. The force behind the spear punched through its scales quite easily and Seth watched as it hurled out of the sky towards the ground. On impact black flames exploded outward torching the forest that was just beyond the wall.

"Be careful everyone, these things explode when they die!" Seth shouted. No sooner had he shouted that than a trail of black fire was laid across the battlements. Several agents scattered including Seth as fire rained down. The fire was so close that Seth could feel the hairs under his gauntlet begin to steam. As he looked down, he realized his armor was doing just that, steaming. And it seemed he would get no chance to recover as he was hit by a sudden impacted that sent him, stones from the wall, and most of the agents around him flying. Seth felt a jarring impact on the side of his helmet, and he realized he was laying on the ground black fire covered everything, and Seth heard the screams of those around him. As Seth shook his head, he forced himself onto one knee as he tried to take stock of the situation. The first thing he noticed was that the nearest ballistae had exploded, and the shrapnel and secondary explosion had been what had hit him and his squad. The second thing Seth noticed was a dragon baring down on him from above, it's maw opening to belch its deadly fire. Seth raised his hand a willed a shield of shimmering light at least a school bus in length to appear.

The fire blast slammed into Seth's shield with the force of freight train, but his shield held. The agents around him had had yet to recover, some weren't moving (Seth was trying not to think about what happened to them). The rest were getting to their feet slowly. The dragon continued its assault on his shield forcing Seth back onto both knees as the force bearing down on him intensified. Seth put more power into the shield and could feel the energy drain from him as he put everything he had into that shield. Unfortunately, he was still a little bit drained from training so he knew he couldn't hold on for much longer. Suddenly more energy was added to the shield and Seth turned around to see an agent on his knees his armor was smoking, and he was bleeding from a wound on his head, but his eyes were focused, his hand outstretched feeding energy to the shield. His other hand was trying to staunch the bleeding from his head.

Seth felt the load lessen once again as another agent was able to rally this one was quite young barely older than fifteen.

"Together!" Seth yelled over the roars in the sky. Seth saw both of them begin to move towards him their armor clanking as they struggled to move. The shield widened to encompass the entire area that they were in. The heat of the black fire lessened and Seth felt less pressure as the dragon veered off to attack some other place on the wall.

"Thanks," Seth muttered between deep heavy breaths. The older agent just nodded but the younger agent managed a smile.

"This is insane!" He said. Then his smile faded as he looked around him. Seth lowered the shield and the brilliant light faded and Seth's world darkened as that light was replaced with the flood lights and torches upon the wall. Seth had to quickly take stock of the current situation as Strat was nowhere to be found. Agents were laying injured all over the wall, there were only about forty or so agents that were rallying. The situation was grim. Seth looked around hoping to spot Strat and have him take command of the agents, but he couldn't see any sign of him. In that moment Seth reacted to the situation.

"Alright who is the highest-ranking agent here besides me," he exclaimed looking from left to right out over the agents assembled in front of him.

"I am!" A man yelled from the back of the group. He pushed his way forward until Seth could see him in the Torchlight. He was a short man probably only five foot eight, but he had a fierceness in his eyes. He has a scruffy black beard and under his helmet Seth spotted slicked back black hair. Seth pointed to him "what's your name?" He asked.

"I am Lutinent Honslo of the Bannot Battalion. I'm Lord Bannot's second in command." He replied strongly.

He'll do, Seth thought to himself.

"Have you seen Strat then?" The man shook his head.

"Not since the explosion, I think he might've been knocked over the wall. Seth's heart dropped to his feet but Honslo simply shrugged. "Knowing him though, he's just fine." Seth realized he was right; no mere fall could kill Strat. Seth had to focus right now on driving off the dragons. Just as Seth was about to start issuing orders a yell came from the staircase to the wall. Seth moved toward it fearing that the demons had broken through somewhere else but he paused when he realized it was his name an agent was calling. The boy was young obviously no older than twelve, but he was clutching his right shoulder in pain and screaming Seth's name from the bottom of the stairs.

Seth turned to Honslo.

"Take command here," he said and then rushed down the stairs to the agent.

The agent was obviously panicking he was looking around frantically and when he spotted Seth, he ran over to him.

"Oh! Thank God I found you." He said the urgency in his voice picking up.

"You're injured agent you need to get to the medical station," Seth said. The agents simply waved his hand as if he wasn't important.

"No time for that I need you to follow me to the West gate."

"Why?" Seth asked his curiosity piqued. Had something gone wrong at the western gate. "Which Battalion are you from?" But Seth knew the answer to both the minute the words left his mouth. He wasn't sure how he knew, he just did.

"I'm from your mother's unit," he said.

"She's in danger of being overrun!"

Chapter 8: Capture

Katie:

Only minutes after the battle had started an explosion rocked the West gate. Katie whose unit had been stationed there immediately went on high alert. But instead of manning the walls they stayed in the street ready to ambush anything or anyone who attempted to come over the wall. And over the wall they did come, an armies worth roughly four hundred demons swarmed over the wall. Katie and her Battalion opened fire launching streams of bolts at the dark fiends. But like always the demons pushed through the attack regardless of their losses. Katie already knew why the demons were there, but it really drove it home when she spotted the black hooded figure Seth had described coming over the wall. It was then she turned to Oscar a small twelve-year-old agent who was still in training at the academy.

"Oscar, I need you to do something for me okay." The little boy whose face had gone pale as the demons came running down the staircase towards them. Their cruel faces filled with excitement as they tore into the first of Katie's men.

"Oscar, I need you to do something for me okay?" Oscar nodded.

Now this is really important I need you to go to the north wall and tell my son Lord Malcovitch that I need help. Can you do that?" The little boy nodded.

"And this is the important part. If when you come back, and I'm not here, tell my son to go to see Barbratoss. That it's very important. Got it?" Once again the little boy nodded."

"Alright get going." Katie instructed.

The little boy turned to go but then stopped.

"What about you?" he asked. Katie smiled at him and then stood to her full height.

"Well," she said drawing her sword I'm going to go do my job." She said calmly blocking a Demon claw as it descended toward her face. Without much thought she flicked the claw away from her and then brought her sword back around and cut down the demon. All without looking away from the boy.

"Now you go okay." The boy didn't say anymore he simply turned and ran.

Katie took a deep breath as she turned to face the enemy in front of her. Her silver katana flashed and the demon in front of her was cut in twain it's challenge roar cut short as he fell in two pieces. Black blood splashed on Katie's armor as she continued her onslaught. The next demon charged slashing at her with a spear made of darkness. Katie responded, she jumped up over the spear lashing out with her sword at the same time to take the enemy's head. More blood spattered her armor as she moved steadily toward the black figure. She cut down everything in her path as she moved forward many of her agents rallying around her. The black swordsman raised his head to look at her, but Katie realized he wore a mask a silver mask with the face of a ghoul the mask had black etched designs in it that sent shivers down Katie's spine.

"So, you must be the black swordsman?" Katie called raising her sword in a challenge. The hooded figure didn't respond he simply readied his sword and closed with her. Katie's last thoughts as she closed with her enemy was of her son and if he would be up for the mission that would surely ensue.

Seth

As Seth was led through the streets of the Academy towards the west gate. He was frantically, trying to rack his brain to figure out why the demons had targeted his mother. But the more he thought of it the more he couldn't understand why it had to be her. Sure, she was a powerful fighter and a leader in the academies but to attack the entire academy just as a distraction to get her. What had his mother done to warrant such attention? Just thinking of it sent shivers down his spine.

"Just got to make it to her before it's too late." Seth kept repeating to himself as they ran down the street. It was only a few minutes later when the horror of what was happening hit home. A black cloaked man was attacking, most likely the same swordsman that tried to kill him and Isbis in Gleamwood, Seth picked up the speed. His mom could handle herself in most situations but this, this was something on a whole other level. Seth had to get to her...now!

As they rounded the last corner following young Oscar what they saw made Seth stop immediately. Agents lay wounded up and down the street, demons still dissipating lay dead surrounding a small group of heavily wounded but still standing agents who stood in the middle of the street. Oscar who obviously recognized one of them took off toward a tall man in his mid-thirties with a Viking style braided beard.

"Lutinent Carthway I brought Master Malcovitch here are you guys doing okay?" Oscar yelled as Seth focused on trying to check the agents laying around him for the face of his mother. Not seeing her he ran to the Lutinent.

"Lutinent! Where is my mother!" Seth exclaimed frantically. But the immediate look of guilt that darkened the man's face told Seth everything.

"They took her sir." Those words hit Seth like horse and all the air rushed out of him as he collapsed onto his knees, the horror evident on his face.

Scenarios ran through Seth's mind of all the things the demons could and might do to his mother.

"I... I have to find her," Seth stammered stumbling to his feet. "If I go after them now, I can catch up to them and..."

"And what?" The Lutinent asked. "There was at least a platoon of them. I don't care how skilled you are you won't come away from that unscathed. and neither will your mother.

"So, what do you expect me to do!" Seth shouted for the first time in a while true anger had washed over him. The Lutinent sighed and put a hand on Seth's shoulder. Before Seth could push him away, he said.

"Look, you mom will be safe for now." Looked at him sharply.

"And how do you know that?" He asked.

"They came here for your mom, right? So, she must have something they want and since they didn't kill her before they took her, you can assume that they need her alive to get it." At those words Seth felt himself relax a little. The man was right, if it was intel, they wanted they would have to keep her alive, which gave Seth time to find her. Seth felt someone tap him on the back and he turned to see Oscar standing there.

"Master Malcovitch?"

"Yeah?" Seth asked, "What is it?

"I have a message for you,"

"For me? Can it wait?" The little boy looked down at his boots.

"Well, uh, um... It was from your mother the commander." Seth's anger escaped from him and he turned on Oscar.

"Well why didn't you tell me before! Spit it out!" The kid shuddered like he was being jabbed with a needle.

"W... well sir she told me to tell you to go see master Barbratoss if something happened to her.

"Barbratoss?" Seth asked.

"Yes sir!" The kid said. "She said it was very important." Seth thought for a moment. If his mother had left this message knowing she would probably be captured, then there had to be a reason. Perhaps it was related to the reason she had been targeted by the Demons.

"Okay!" Seth said, "We have a battle to finish, but after we are done I'm going to go have a little chat with Barbratoss and then go save my mother." Seth stared pointedly at the Lutinent.

"One way or the other."

Chapter 9: The Whereabouts of the Gems

It didn't take long to finish the battle. By the time Seth had arrived back on the scene the dragons had already pulled out and were already far away. Now began the long process of rebuilding and taking care of the wounded. But Seth wasn't interested in any of that. While he felt for those hurt in the battle, now he had a singular goal: find his mother at least what she had been hiding.

The evacuation of all the wounded had been well underway by the time Seth had arrived at Barbratoss' humble abode. As Seth was about to knock on the door, the door was swung wide open and Seth almost didn't have time to dodge the axe that came flying out. Having no time to throw up a shield of light Seth threw himself backward in a summersault the axe narrowly missing his head as he did.

The axe embedded itself three inches into a boulder on the other side of the clearing that surrounded Barbratoss' house. Seth drew his sword as he stood but almost immediately lowered it when he recognized the owner of the axe. Barbratoss stood there in the doorway of his home another axe already ready to throw. However, recognizing who it was Seth saw Barbratoss lower his axe.

"Boy? Is that you?"

"Yes, it's me, Put down the axe!" Seth exclaimed sheathing Sonfang. Barbratoss hesitated for a moment but then put down the axe.

"So, they captured her didn't they?" He asked. The question completely threw Seth off.

"Wait you knew this would happen?" Seth demanded. The old dwarf solemnly shook his head.

"No, I didn't know it would, but we always knew it could happen which is why she told me that if after the battle if you came to see me before she did that she had most likely been captured."

"Wait, by her you mean my mother?"

"Of course, that's who I mean. We also thought they might come after me so that is why... Anyway, sorry for the axe." Seth dusted himself off as he gestured with his head toward the door.

"Can I come in? I think we have a lot to talk about." Barbratoss nodded.

"Yes, you can and Yes we do." He turned and went inside and left Seth to follow.

After they were inside Barbratoss motioned toward the table with his hand. "Sit, you must have a lot of questions." Seth sat in the seat the dwarf had indicated and awaited Barbratoss to start talking. Barbratoss eyed Seth up and down before he began to speak.

"You know, I have never been one to talk in rhymes, so I'll come out and say it. The thing me and your mom were hiding was the location of the air gem." Seth was on his feet in seconds.

"What!?"

"I told you I wasn't much of a storyteller, but I guess that was a little too much straight to the point, eh?" Seth nodded and took his seat again.

"If you guys knew the location of the Air Gem then why you didn't reveal this information to Samson and Strat?" The dwarf sighed as he reached onto the table to a long silver pitcher with a long pouring neck. He grabbed it and stood up and walked into what Seth could only guess was his version of a kitchen. He reached into the cupboards and withdrew two silver cups but hesitated before he could fully pull them out.

"Would you like some ale?"

"No," Seth said. "I'm still underage."

"Right," Barbratoss said as he poured himself a glass. "I forgot you still cling to the rules of Terra."

"Terra?" Seth asked. Another sigh.

"That's what we dwarves call the normal world." Barbratoss sat back down this time cup in hand. he took a sip. "To answer your question. Because we felt it was not yet time to reveal such information. Your mother was tasked by a certain angel to protect and hide away the air gem."

"An angel? for real?"

"Yes, we can see angels here. You didn't know that? They usually appear with a message from God, so when one arrives it is of the utmost importance. However, this one appeared in secrecy to only three people me and your mother were two of those people."

"Anyway, my mother had instructed me to come see you. What do you know?" Seth only needed a moment to process all that had been said before he continued. "You were entrusted with the whereabouts of the air gem, weren't you?!" Barbratoss shook his head.

"No! Not me, but I do know who knows where it lies."

"Who?" Seth asked anxiously. Seth saw the fleeting but still very clear moment of hesitation before he answered.

"Stevos Arnoclaee," he said finally. The name only served to confuse Seth further.

"And who is that."

"The king of the elves," Barbratoss answered.

"You know you'll have to report this with me to the war council, right?" Seth said. Barbratoss raised his tankard and down the last several gulps of ale in one go.

"Yeah, I know," He said grimly as he rose from his seat. "Well better get to it we both have important things to do." Seth rose as well recognizing that the war council would have already started by now.

By the time Seth and Barbratoss had arrived at the council chambers the session had been well underway. Samson stood as Seth entered the room a look of worry on his face. The same look that was shared around the room.

"Seth, are you sure you should be here right now?" Samson asked the tone of his voice made it clear to Seth that he should leave if he couldn't keep his cool, but Seth simply replied.

"I don't know where else I'd be. Besides I have some new information that has come to light."

"And what information is that, a burly man said from where he sat beside Samson.

Seth recognized him as Johnathan Mackson the new leader of the nature academy.

"I'll let Barbratoss explain." Seth said as he backed away and let Barbratoss into the room. Strat who was sitting to the right of Samson a clear charred smell coming off his armor leaned forward.

"What do you have for us Master Barbratoss."

After the explanation, there was complete shock emanated from all the council members. Matt was the first to respond.

"The air gem! And its location was right under our noses. Why didn't she tell us."? Strat stood and began to pace.

"We can't blame her, from what you've said Barbratoss she had very specific orders from the angel. And we are bound to follow those orders. So, it makes since that not even we were made aware." Matt nodded.

"Makes sense."

"So, our mission is clear now, we will send the Disciples to collect the Air gem." Samson said standing as well. He turned to Strat.

"Are you and Jack going to tag along again?" Strat turned to face Samson a resolute expression on his face.

"Yes, I am I can't speak for Jack, but I am because I'm going to be continuing Seth's training." Samson raised an eyebrow.

"Master Seth has learned to master water and is very capable with most of the elements but he still has much to learn and relies on his power far too much." Seth looked down slightly embarrassed, but the feeling only worsened when John laughed.

"Well," he said "if you are headed to elven lands, you'll be passing through the nature academies territory you'll need a guide. Lucky for you, I'd be happy to help."

John was a burly man who looked more likely to cut down a tree than grow one, but he was talented. At Only thirty-three he was a giant of a man standing over six foot tall, with black sleeked back hair and a full but trimmed beard for someone who lived in the wild he looked very refined. His Olive skin served to further this sentiment but the wild look in his eyes told a very different story. He wore the standard white plate and chainmail armor.

"Okay," Samson said clapping his hands together "we are in agreement. Seth Strat and master Jack if he so chooses will accompany the disciples on their mission to recover the air gem and save Chief Commander Malcovitch!"

Chapter 10: Set off from the North Gate

Stratos Bannot

As Seth and the others were leaving the Council chambers Strat reached out his hand to stop Seth who paused.

"What's up?" Seth asked. Strat thought about how he should put his questions into words.

"I guess I was just wondering if you're okay." Strat watched as Seth almost scowled.

"No, how could I be okay," Seth said in a controlled voice. Strat could tell that Seth was restraining himself quite a bit.

"I do have a question for you though." Strat motioned for Seth to walk with him which he did.

"Okay, what's the question?"

"What happened to you during the battle? Where did you go?" Strat paused for a moment embarrassed. It was one thing to get caught up in the heat of battle, but I was another thing to not keep your cool and get blasted from the battlements.

"As embarrassing as it is to say this, I spent to majority of the battle at the bottom of the wall dodging fire blasts. Dragons and I don't really get along and I'm afraid they haven't forgotten who I am.

"And just who are you to them?" Seth asked.

Strat shrugged not feeling like telling Seth yet another legend about him.

"Let me guess you are the bane of all dragons as well." Again, Strat shrugged.

"Something like that." Strat followed Seth as they exited the HQ and began the trek down to the city towards their respective houses. They were to depart immediately after all.

When they arrived at the intersection to split off. Strat grabbed Seth's shoulder and turned him towards him. Strat could see the worry in his eyes. Seth was very close to tears. Strat turned to Seth and looked at him in the eyes.

"Don't worry Seth, we'll find your mother." Seth pushed Strat away playfully.

"I know we will," he said. "We have to, or I don't know what I'll do."

After Strat had finished packing, he stepped outside his home. He lived in a small, gated manor that had six bedrooms, three bathrooms, a common room, a living room, a kitchen and a guest kitchen. And two dining rooms. Did he need a house so extravagant? Not one bit, in fact he was hardly ever home because it felt so empty. However, it was the house of his station and after many agents telling him to accept it, even going so far as to try to move his stuff in the middle of the night, Strat had just given in to it. But as he exited his house wearing his usual brown cloak over chainmail and plate armor, he was greeted by Jack who was waiting by the front gate.

Strat hardly even looked up he was used to Jack enough that he had known jack had been outside his house for almost thirty minutes.

"So, you are tagging along too," Jack said in is normal smooth voice.

"Yeah, and you," Strat replied. Jack brushed his long black hair out of his eyes and motioned with his head to a couple of bags sitting by the wall. Strat didn't fail to notice there was no sword on his hip though.

"What about your weapon?" Strat asked.

"I'm not bringing it," Jack replied simply. "I'm trying to train myself to not rely on physical weapons and instead be ready with a light sword at a moment's notice." Strat shrugged.

"Whatever you got to do, man."

"You know, you should cut that hair," Strat said and Jack finally cracked a smile. That was the side of Jack that almost no one else ever got to see. They would always see the cautious, quiet, mysterious Jack. But most people had no idea he actually had a great sense of humor.

"Yeah but at least, I have hair," jack retorted.

"I have hair, it's just not as long as your entire mane of hair!" Jack laughed as he began to walk towards the gate. Strat followed close behind.

"We better get down to the stables so we can be ready to leave as soon as possible," Strat said. They walked for some time in silence as they both made their way towards the north bound gate.

"You know Strat, if we are going to go visit Stevos shouldn't you tell Seth."

Strat thought about what Jack was saying, after all it was a delicate matter.

"No, it's better to wait and see if His Majesty wants to reveal it or not. If not, I'll tell Seth anyway because he has the right to know."

"Well that very contradictory of you," Jack said.

"Yeah, well I've given Stevos the benefit of the doubt, so he better not let me down." Jack sighed.

"That's not exactly what I meant, but we don't have time to worry about it now, I have to take this time to prepare for the journey." Strat nodded as they approached the northern gate. In the middle of the brick paved road that exited the north gate stood Seth and the others, most on horseback. As Strat approached Seth let go of a lead that led to a beautiful white mare. She was packed for travel already with every necessity they might need. Blankets, fire starter, rope, stakes, even a couple of pots.

"Well Seth it seems I get to thank you for saving me a trip to the stables." Strat told him as he swiftly mounted his horse. From behind Seth Strat saw Matt snicker.

Seth said nothing as he turned away from Strat a deadly serious expression on his face.

"We need to get going, we have a long way to go and we need to hurry, my mother is waiting." Jack mounted his horse as well and Strat caught the look he was throwing at Seth and Strat understood it.

This wasn't like Seth at all. Normally he would've made some quip about how late Strat always was, but not today. There was no trace of Seth's usual joking Self. Behind Seth, Matt, Mike, Johnathan, Rylee, Travice, Michelle, and Aria all sat quietly on their horses. Only Rylee and Michelle seemed unaffected by the mood Seth was putting out. That was probably due to them being focused staring at a map of the northern academy lands.

"Alright, you're right we should be going we have a long way to travel before night falls again," Strat said in resignation. As he passed Travice the scout of the group turned stopped Strat with a hand.

"Is Seth going to be okay?" He asked. "This isn't like him." Strat gave him a reassuring smile.

"He'll be fine. It will just take him some time." Travice nodded concern etched into his face.

"I hope so..."

However, as they left the north gate, fires still burning across it, Strat had to admit he wasn't so sure.

Chapter 11: The Cost

They were over an hour into their journey. The sun just coming over the horizon when Seth spoke to the group. Seth had been holding in a lot of emotions in the hours since his mother had been taken, but these were his friends he needed to at least tell them what was going on Inside his head. The chill of the morning air was causing the whole group to move slower than usual, so Seth decided to use this moment to get his emotions off his chest.

"You know guys, I'm not meaning to be rude or anything, I just have a lot on my mind." The whole group paused, and it felt as if they all simultaneously looked back at him.

"Well, that was random," Matt said as he wheeled his horse around to face Seth. The smirk he always wore evident on his face. At this even Aria cracked a smile

"You pick the weirdest times to talk about your feeling," Travice said.

"How about you hear him out before you start telling him how weird he is." Seth turned around to see Rylee trot her horse up alongside his. She turned to Seth encouragingly. Seth heard a scoff come from Jack's direction, but he continued.

"I know it's not like me to be quiet, but I have a lot on my mind. To find out my mother was the demons target was surprising enough, but then to find out that she was hiding one of the gems we've been searching for this entire time and didn't tell us. It got me confused. It made me wonder what else she could be..."

"She had to have her reasons," Strat interrupted.

"Yeah, the commander never did anything without a reason," Michelle stated.

"Well, I don't know her like you guys do," Travice said. "But from what I have seen of her I would agree with what Michelle said. John muscled his way in between Rylee and Seth's horses

"Yeah, well I think this little pity party is a waste of time," Johnathan said as he willed his horse forward, past Seth and the others. A twinge of anger touched Seth and he struggled to push it down. Seth noticed that everyone in the group was throwing looks at John's back.

Seth was about to say something back when a smell wafted across his senses. He immediately gagged. It was a horrible smell, but one Seth unfortunately knew. And it seemed like he wasn't the only one who noticed it. The others had begun to take notice as well. It was the smell of decay. One so profound that Seth instantly knew that it was the smell of death.

"This can't be good," Rylee stated a look of worry replaced the smile she had just before. Seth turned to Strat who had already turned very serious.

"Travice, Matt I need you to scout ahead," Strat created a light sword, appearing in his hands in a flash of light Seth also drew his weapon. Readying himself for an attack at any time.

"We'll go in safely. I already think I know where the smell is coming from, but it doesn't hurt to be careful. But we need to hurry.

Seth heard the gallop of Travice's horse as he came flying back toward them. When he was still about thirty feet away, he stopped and cupped his hands around his mouth.

"You guys need to come see this now!" He exclaimed clearly shaken. Even from thirty feet away Seth could tell Clovis was trembling. He wasn't the only one who saw it either.

"Ha!" Strat exclaimed as he dug his heels into his horse. The horse took off past Seth and Seth followed suit.

The sight that greeted them when they came over the last hill to overlook a tiny farmstead shook Seth to the core. It wasn't right to call it a village for it was just a collection of tiny houses arranged in a circle and surrounded by a fence. At least it had been a Farmstead, now it was in ruins. Every house was on fire or in smoldering ruins. But that wasn't the worst part, the worst part was the bodies. At least a hundred bodies were strewn all over the area. children, adults, and even the elderly, no one had been spared. Their faces still frozen in the fear they felt in the moment of their death. Blood splattered all over the valley. Seth immediately heaved. He'd seen death last year when Isbis died and again on the wall against the demon dragons. But nothing like this. Everyone in the academies understood the risks of what they did. But these people, they weren't given that chance.

"Whoa...," Rylee gulped.

"But why?" Aria asked solemn hands covering her mouth. Seth looked back at Strat and a dark shadow had come over his face and even from where Seth was, he could see Strat trembling with anger.

Seth took a deep breath and gathered himself. "I'm going down there," he said.

"Why," Travice asked unlike the rest of them there was no indication that what he was seeing was affecting him.

"I'm going to check for survivors," Seth answered simply and without waiting for a response he headed into the valley of death.

Seth passed several bodies on his way into the farmstead all of them killed mercilessly. a mother still clutched the body of her now dead daughter. Seth turned away from the sight a cold feeling gathered in his stomach as he realized for the first time that what he was looking at was the cost. the cost of war the cost of protecting. He also realized in that moment that these people were all good people, not perfect but who is. As Seth picked his way past a charred fence into the ring of burning houses the smoke became more evident and Seth was forced to cover his face with his arm. it was then that he saw that the people had tried to fight back. At the first house he came to the wood of the house had unnaturally twisted into a noose. hanging in that noose was the dead body of a demon. it wasn't like the demons Seth had seen before. It was skinnier more haggard, and even though it was clearly dead Seth could still see intelligence hidden deep within its eyes.

"Help," a weak voice gasped. Shock ran through Seth as he realized that it had come from a collapsed house nearby.

"Where are you," Seth exclaimed as he ran toward the house immediately drawing upon his earthen abilities as he ran. A gust of wind hit the ground behind Seth and Seth turned to see Strat and Jack landing behind him, they must've heard his yell. The house they were approaching was partially collapsed and luckily this one hadn't burned completely. The voice had come from the only part of the house that wasn't on fire, one of the bedrooms.

"Seth, put out the fire!" Jack ordered. Seth didn't even think. He began to glow as water shot from his hand in a torrent. The fire sizzled and cracked as his water met it. Seth began to extinguish the fire, but it was taking longer than he had expected. Seth was very careful to put out the fire closest to the unburned part first. As he worked, he heard Jack giving other orders as Strat was busy clearing the smoke out of the air and continually funneling the smoke away from the room.

"John can you pull down the wall farthest from the fire?" Jack asked.

"Absolutely, Let's get them out of there," John said all traces of his earlier arrogance now gone. Seth did his best to focus as he widened the spray of the water shooting from his hand. Seth reached deeper and the torrent of water exploded. Water began to fall from the sky drenching everything. Rain? Seth thought in the back of his head. But there aren't even any clouds. Seth momentarily looked up to see where the water was coming from and the rain was just falling from the sky. there were no clouds at all rain was falling in a torrent out of the blue sky. When all the fire in the village had gone out Seth loosened his hold on the power gradually letting it go. The rain stopped almost at once as Seth felt the power leave him. Seth turned around and saw his friends surrounding a couple of little kids. One was a red headed girl. She seemed to be older than the little boy she was clutching to her chest. the boy looked up from her embrace fearfully. Seth walked up with a smile on his face not sure if he had scared the kids or if the demons had.

"Well nice of you to join us Seth," Strat said. "You went a little too, deep didn't you?" he asked.

Seth simply nodded not knowing what he was talking about. Strat obviously realized that Seth didn't know what he meant so he waved it away.

Seth hurried over to see them. The minute he got to close the girl quailed, screaming something intelligible and releasing a wave of fire, Seth quickly jumped back and drew upon his power of fire. The fire passed harmlessly around him. the others similarly blocked the wave of fire.

"We think she has long since lost consciousness, she's just doing this out of the pure will to defend her brother. The little boy coughed violently and Seth could see blood come out as well. but still the little boy looked up at him.

"Please don't hurt my sis, she is only trying to protect me." Seth smiled at him trying to put him at ease.

"We would never hurt your sister, but we do need to wake her up so we can take care of you two. Just sit still, we will take care of this." Seth studied her closely and could plainly tell she had lost consciousness. "We are trying to approach her without her going all "flame on" on us", Aria stated. Seth felt something in the pit of his stomach as he realized what this little girl must have gone through. Parents dead, demons overrunning her home, her brother clinging to her afraid, looking to her for protection. This was something no girl her age should be worried about.

"It must've been hard on you until now," He said as he began to walk forward.

"What are you doing Seth, we just told you she won't let any-one approach."

Once again, the wave of fire came outward from her and this time Seth reached inward and the fire dissipated before it ever reached him. Seth knelt and wrapped his arms around the young girl and her charge. At first, she resisted him trying to activate her power however Seth had successfully created a field around her to immediately dissipate any fire she would unleash.

"It's okay now, you are safe," Seth said softly to the young girl. Almost Immediately the attempts at using her power faltered, and Seth could tell the girl was regaining consciousness. the girl's eyes opened and Seth let the girl go as she shuffled backward from him still dragging her injured younger brother with her. Bewilderment and shock were written all over her face as she clearly struggled to figure out what had happened to her. Then there was pain in her eyes and tears welled up as she began to sob quietly at first but with growing intensity. Seth stepped toward her again and she seemed to recognize the fact that Seth and his friends were there. Seth knelt next to her.

"Listen, I know you have been through a lot but we need to know if you or your brother are hurt." Seth waited for the sniffling to stop and for the girl to answer. She looked up at him with fear still very present in her eyes.

"Who are you guys?" She asked.

"We are from the Lightforce Academy," Strat said as he walked slowly up to her. He materialized a blanket out of thin air and wrapped it around her shoulders. Her eyes went wide at the mention of the Academy and she immediately grabbed Seth's hand. she moved so fast that Seth didn't have time to react.

"Please, you can save my little brother then can't you!" She exclaimed. She laid her brother down in front of her and Seth immediately could tell that the child was in danger. A small Rectangular stab wound was located just under the boys ribs. Blood had soaked the entire front of the young boy's shirt. The boy looked up at his sister, he couldn't have been, more than nine years old but the caring look he gave his sister was obviously one of someone that knew he was dying.

"Sis I'll be okay. I'll see mama and papa soon again." Seth glanced up at Strat who had a dark expression on his face. Strat shook his head slowly; the boy was beyond their help. The boy looked up at Seth pain and tears welling up as he now struggled to speak.

"Thank you for saving my sister, but I have a request of you." Seth knelt beside the boy and grabbed his tiny hand in his.

"Don't worry we will take care of your sister; you don't have to worry little one."

"Isn't there anything we can do?" Seth heard Rylee ask Strat.

"No, he's already lost too much blood and even if we use our bandages to close the wound, he is still bleeding from internal bleeding," Michelle answered for him.

"Come on you guys can save him right!?" The girl yelled desperation entering her voice. Seth felt the tears well up in his own eyes at the little boys next words.

"Have faith sis, it's too late for me but you will see me again, I'll just be waiting with mama and papa." The little boy's strength and maturity hurt Seth to the core. No kid should have to endure this.

"But...But you'll be leaving me alone, I don't want you to go," The girl sobbed. The boy's eyes began to lose their glint and his labored breathing increased. He gripped Seth's hand tightly.

"It hurts," he said tears in his eyes. Seth wiped tears from his eyes with one of his hands.

"Don't worry it'll be over soon," He managed. Seth looked up at his friends. Every one of them were wearing the same pained look he knew was probably on his face as well. Rylee, Aria and Matt were even crying tears streaming down their faces. Suddenly the boys hand went slack, and Seth couldn't explain how but, in that moment,

he knew the boy had just died.

Chapter 12: Rest

That Day they spent burying the dead population of the farmstead. They decided to camp on the hill that was overlooking the valley. Nobody talked much especially Seth. The little girl had helped bury her brother, and her parents but afterwards she sat down where her brother had died and wouldn't move. she just stared at the bloodstained ground unmoving. The only thing They could get out of her was her name, Rubia. As Seth stared at the little girl full of pain his own heart broke yet again. Seth went to go comfort her but felt Strat's hand on his shoulder.

"Seth, we need someone to go get firewood and she could use time to herself," he said. Seth didn't reply he simply nodded and left. As Seth was gathering firewood he heard voices in the brush near the farmstead. It piqued his interest only because as far as he knew he was the only one in the farmstead, everyone else had gone up to the hill camp. Seth crouched down as he tried to approach without being heard. As he neared the voices stopped abruptly before he could hear what was being said. Seth stood up ready to rush in, but he ran right into Travice and Aria who were coming out of the brush.

"Seth, what are you doing down here," Aria asked quickly straightening up.

"Looking for firewood," Seth replied. "The question is why are you here?" Aria looked down and then glanced at Travice. "Do we tell him," She asked. Travice threw her an angered look.

"Well, we don't have a choice now, Do we?" He replied clearly annoyed. Seth furrowed his eyebrows in suspicion. He quickly flashed back to Strat telling him that there were traitors within the academy. Seth subtly dropped into a defensive stance ready for anything. After all Strat had specifically said not to trust anyone.

"With how you've been lately we weren't going to tell you right away, but it seems we have no choice," Travice said.

"Tell me what?" Seth asked his suspicion rising.

Travice sighed.

"The band of demons that attacked this village wasn't random," he said solemnly as he did, he pulled out a sheathed silver katana. Seth knew it was his mother's instantly. The weapon along with his was one of a kind. It was about three feet of curved conoroid the strongest metal known to them. It was trimmed in white gold around the hilt and pummel and the guard was fashioned with a gold dragon encircling the blade forever cursed to try and consume itself. The handle itself was wrapped in literal dragon leather which was extremely rare considering dragons were considered extinct a fact that Seth had only recently learned. Seth ran his hands over the graceful weapon. He took the blade from Travice and turned it over in his hands admiring the words etched in the sheath.

"We don't know what those words say since we can't read them..." Travice said.

"By the grace of God we rise," Seth said almost as an afterthought.

"Huh?" Aria asked confused.

"It's what it says on here," Seth added for context. Travice frowned then his face cleared.

"Oh, you mean your mother told you what it says." Seth shook his head.

"No, I can read it why can't you it's just English." the confusion was evident in their faces.

Travice turned the blade's sheath and took a closer look at it, his confusion obviously only deepening. "No, I can read English but this..." He said pointing at the words that looked like clear English to Seth.

"This is Elvish," He finished. Now it was Seth's turn to be confused.

"What are you talking about," Seth said. Travice shook his head.

"it doesn't matter we need to get back to camp because tomorrow we will be crossing into the Elvish lands and we need to be ready for that.

As they were walking back to camp Seth leaned over and whispered to Aria.

"What's so different about the Elvish lands compared to our own. Aria smiled at him.

"That's right sometimes I forget you aren't from our world," she said. Seth felt his face flush at that. but she quickly threw her hands up waving frantically.

"It's nothing to be embarrassed about after all the fact that you have had the outside influences is one of the things that makes you so powerful, but naturally in return there are things about our world you wouldn't know. Anyway, let me explain it to you. The Elven lands to put it simply are in a state of chaos. Unlike in the Academy lands, demons pretty much run rampant in the other lands. Especially in the Elven lands. Seth took a moment to let this sink in.

"Wait weren't the Elves the Protectors of Elementia before the Lightforce?" Aria nodded.

"Yeah, they were, but then they were replaced by the Lightforce Academy about 2,000 years ago."

"Okay but still if they were once the protectors of Elementia how could they let demons run rampant in their territory. Do they not care?" Aria shook her head.

"It's not that, there is just not enough of them and their abilities are too limited." Seth cast a confused glance at Aria.

"What do you mean there is not enough of them?" Aria blushed.

"The birth rate of elves is extremely low. They only have a max of two children their entire lives. And that's if they are lucky."

"Oh," Seth replied turning away.

They arrived back at camp, just as John returned to camp with an armful of wood he stopped as Seth and his group entered camp. Seth watched as John eyed them suspiciously. Seth ignored him and went into the camp to a slight cliff that overlooked the valley. Up on it Strat sat alone. Ever since he had told Seth to go get firewood, Strat had sat up here. he hadn't talked to anyone not even Jack. Seth walked up behind him careful not to disturb him. Seth sat down next to Strat and crossed his legs. He put his mother's sword across his legs and turned to look at Strat. His eyes were closed as if he was focusing on something. Seth realized that he was praying. His lips moved silently, uttering a prayer Seth could not hear. Seth waited patiently for Strat to finish. It didn't take long, Strat opened his eyes and glanced at Seth from the corner of his eye. He nodded once acknowledging that Seth was there, but continued looking straight forward, the boy's death was bothering him. Not that Seth could blame him. Strat took any death he couldn't prevent as a personal strike against him. It was a part of him being the protector, a role he took seriously.

"So," Seth began.

"It was the group of demons who captured your mom wasn't it?" Strat finished. Seth stared at him dumbfounded.

"How did you?"

"Because" Strat interrupted as he stood up and began brushing of his armor. "It is their only tactical option when it comes to getting us off their trail. They know us well; we wouldn't just ignore something like this." Seth stood as well holding out his mother's katana for Strat to take, however Strat raised his hand to stop him. "Keep it with you. Me and you both know she would want you to keep a hold of it." Seth nodded and slipped the sword into his belt on the opposite hip that Sonfang was on.

"Thanks, "Seth muttered. Strat shook his head.

"No need to thank me man, let's just make sure we get to hand it back to her personally." Seth nodded. Strat turned back towards camp to leave but before he did, he laid a hand on Seth's shoulder. "Go and get some rest. Starting tomorrow we are going to be seeing plenty of action so you will need your rest. From what I hear until we reach the Elven Capitol of Farthratrost, we will be under constant attack by demons so prepare. Also, I will be assigning you to take care of that little girl, keep her safe." With that Strat turned and walked back towards camp. But Seth stayed out by the cliff for a while longer staring out at the world as the sun showed its last rays. As he marveled at the world, he couldn't help but wonder if he would be able to hand his mother her sword again.

Chapter 13: The Hunters

Stratos Bannot

It only took them one day after entering the Elven lands to come under attack. It was in the morning and they only had half a day's journey left until they made it to the capitol. Strat was watching as his friends break down camp in the shallow wood where they had made camp the night before. the trip so far had remained uneventful and for that Strat was thankful. Strat made himself some coffee from the pot, that Michelle had put on when she had awoken in the morning, filling the entire area with the smell of coffee. Unfortunately, the fire was only smoldering, so the coffee did not get heated all the way. Strat shrugged; a warm coffee was better than no coffee. He was deeply engrossed in thinking about half heated coffee when he felt it through the earth. The vibrations of about a two dozen or more running feet. But these steps were not frantic they were paced and careful. Light steps that were hard to even feel, the steps came from all around their camp and, they travelled only in one direction. Right for the camp. Strat whipped around and his mouth opened to warn his friends of the impending attack, but Seth beat him to it.

Seth

"Incoming," Seth yelled as he pushed Rylee out of the way of a bolt of darkness as it came hurling out of the densely packed forest. It whizzed overhead striking a half taken down tent and exploded. The explosion sent Matt tumbling over the fire pit. In an instant Mike and Jack were on their feet weapons in hand. However, Aria and Michelle were not so lucky. Dark bolts struck the two of them as they came running back towards the center of camp from where they had been loading up the horses. They tumbled to the ground where they laid clothes smoking. Seth raised his left hand and punched the earth and a wall of stone rose out of the ground encircling the camp at about chest height. A moment later a dome of brilliant white light encompassed the encampment as well offering additional protection. Seth grabbed Rylee's hand and pulled her upright as she reached for her weapon.

"Everyone find cover!" Seth heard Strat yell. Seth and Rylee ran for the earthen wall. Seth looked back to see Strat holding up the dome of light as bolts of darkness slammed into it. As each bolt hit the shield, they exploded shaking the ground and deafening Seth with the noise. Seth put his hand out and fired a bolt into the brush where he spotted movement. An unearthly howl erupted, and a demon fell forward through the brush dead. Seth peeked over the barricade to look at the demon he had just felled. Seth had only glimpsed it briefly but what he had seen did not seem right. But as two more bolts flew into his barricade he decided to wait and focus on the battle.

Seth looked out over the encampment trying to locate everyone. Aria and Michelle were still down. Seth felt a twinge of pain as he saw their unmoving bodies. Seth noticed that as a bolt exploded near Aria her hand twitched which meant that they were still alive. Seth scanned the camp to find the one person he was truly worried about, Rubia. It was not long before he spotted her. She was crouched behind a tree tears running down her face as she openly sobbed. Terror was written all over her face as bolts of darkness few in every direction. Standing over her was a kind of demon Seth had never seen before. Seth's first impression of it screamed hunter. it was sleek with longer legs it was less humanoid and instead had the look of a predator. It still stood on two feet with two clawed hands, but its legs boasted powerful hunches that spoke of a speed that other demons did not possess. Its wings were folded along its back and instead of an almost human face it had a long snout, its mouth full of wicked sharp teeth. It wore armor even if it was only black leather chestplate with a thin hood. that only covered half of its snout. The demon was looking down at Rubia with a hunger in its eyes.

"Rubia!" Seth exclaimed as he began to gather his feet beneath him to run to her side. There was no way that Seth was going to let that demon no matter how terrifying it looked, hurt Rubia. But, before Seth could even begin to move Seth heard the distinct sound of a gun being cocked. From over where the horses were, came a flash of light and the demon screamed in pain as it was riddled with holes. In an Instant thick roots began to grow out of the wound and wrap themselves around the demon killing it almost immediately. It fell sideways landing only a few inches from Rubia's terrified face which caused her to scream. Then running across the clearing was

John without any armor and still in his boxers he was holding his

weapon. which much to Seth's surprise seemed to be some kind of

sawed-off shotgun, made of pure silver. Bolts flew at him from every

direction, as he ran, he yelled something that Seth could not make

out as he dove for the tree that Rubia hid behind. He threw himself

into a roll and came up gun at the ready. he pointed his gun at Seth

and fired. For a split-second Seth thought that John had been aiming

for him and he felt his blood chill. But when he fired Seth heard the

scream of a demon from the other side of the earthen barrier. John

scowled at Seth.

"Don't worry about other's focus on yourself! We already have

two down!" Seth nodded realizing he was right. Seth looked to his

right to where Rylee was crouched, she looked over at him as well.

She reached up and pushed a strand of her brown hair out of her eyes.

"He's right you know, "She said in her usual haughty voice.

Seth only smiled and then tried to refocus on the fight. Seth peek over the edge of the barrier trying to get a view of where the enemy was positioned. The first thing he saw was one of the snarling beasts charging straight at his part of the barricade at an impossible speed.

"Oh crap, "Seth said as he quickly raised his hand palm out and fired a bolt of white energy straight at the charging fiend. It reached behind it's back and drew a slim black curved sword, which it used to slash away Seth's bolt of energy. Seth tightened his grip on his sword as he made the split-second decision to hop over the barricade and meet the creature head on.

"Seth! What are you doing!" Rylee exclaimed. Truth was Seth really did not know himself. He could have pretended he had a plan, but he didn't, he was just trying to keep the demons away from the barricade. As Seth engaged the demon another shield of light was erected by Strat over the clearing. But Seth was far too busy to pay attention to that. Seth dove to the right as the snapping jaws of the demon came almost too close to taking a chunk out of his side.

Seth swung Sonfang towards the left side of the creature trying to finish the fight fast but it danced sideways so Seth only succeeded in grazing it. Seth gave chase only to throw himself backward in a summersault as a dark blade whisked over his head. Seth was pretty sure he'd gotten a bit of a hair taken off from that. Seth brought his sword around horizontally and this time he felt Sonfang cut as he decapitated the beast. But Seth did not have time to feel good about his victory because immediately after that Seth was attacked by another demon. Seth parried both enemies blows and the lunged his sword sliding past the demon's guard into its belly. It roared and slashed out with its swords. Seth didn't have time to react, one sword tore open a gash on his thigh while the other one left a sizable cut on his left forearm. Seth felt the pain explode in his body and he had to grit his teeth to keep from crying out as, yet another creature charged at him from the bushes. Seth raised his uninjured right hand and let loose a fury of bolts that knocked the demon to the ground. It slid forward its body smoking it, was dead.

These attacks went on for several minutes before Seth group successfully killed the demons off. Seth stabbed the last on in the gut just as Strat came flying overhead and took the demons head off.

Seth watched Strat land and roll sword at the ready. Then he slowly stood.

He looked at Seth. "That seems to be all of them." He said then a smile broke out on his face. "What a way to wake up huh? Seth willed some bandages to appear and then began wrapping his wounds.

"Yeah, no kidding," He replied grunting as pain erupted from his arm. He was wrapping the bandages as tight as he could. Having to use his teeth to pull the cloth at sometimes. Blood splotches appeared on the clothes covering the wounds. The cuts had been far deeper that Seth had first thought.

"Seth," Strat said. Seth looked up.

"You know we have healing bandages, right?" Seth nodded.

"I do but I have a feeling Aria and Michelle will need those more."

Seth and Strat returned to the clearing to find most of the group were hovered over Aria and Michelle who had been moved and we are now laying on their back side by side near the fire. Both were unconscious and both bore nasty burns. Seth limped into the clearing and kneeled beside Rylee who was trying to apply the Lightforce's healing bandages to the girl's wounds.

"I need you to give me some space," Rylee said without looking at Seth. Her eyes were completely focused on the task. Seth said nothing, he really didn't have the energy to either. So, he struggled back to his feet and shuffled back. Mike came over to him and sat down on the ground next to him. His right pauldron was smoking. He looked up at Seth noticing the wounds.

He raised an eyebrow. "You alright there?" he asked. Seth nodded. "You know if you had been wearing your armor that wouldn't have happened right?" Seth looked down at him to see Mike smiling. Seth cracked a smile himself. Mike's dry humor was always a welcome distraction from his pain. On the other side of the clearing Strat, Jack, John, and Matt were talking, probably trying to figure out the next move now that they had two injured. Matt's hair was definitely singed from his little tumble in the fire pit, and he looked none too pleased about it either. Seth closed his eyes and tried to focus on the earth. Someone had to keep a look out in case there were more of those hunter demons. Sure, enough Seth felt several dozen light footsteps coming straight for them. They were still several miles out, but they were closing fast.

"Strat! We need to leave," Seth yelled. "Now!" Strat looked over at Seth his face a mixture of confusion. Mike also looked up at him clearly confused. Then Seth saw Strat and Jack's faces change.

"No, there's more of them," Jack said clearly distressed. Strat shook his head.

"We need to get the wounded up and on horses now." Rylee's head shot up at that.

"What! Move them, I haven't even begun to treat them if we move them it could make their condition worse." Strat walked over to her and laid a hand on her shoulder looking her in the eyes.

"I don't like it either but right now more enemies are coming, too many to fight. It's either we risk moving them or we all die here." Rylee looked down at Aria and Michelle for a moment and then her shoulder drooped.

"Okay but I need you guys to help me get them up and tied into the saddle. Seth stood up and began to make his way to the horses. Mike ran up behind him and offered a shoulder.

"Here I'll help you get on the horse."

"We need to hurry," Strat said. "Leave anything that isn't important we make for the Elven Capitol!"

Chapter 14: Discovery

Stratos Bannot

Strat was sure that they would not make it. They had been riding hard now for several hours but to no avail. They just couldn't shake their pursuers. They were still several miles from the capitol but more and more of the Shadow Hunters kept showing up. That is what Strat had come to call them. The Shadow Hunters. A totally new class of demon. In all of Strat's two thousand years protecting the academy he had only come across a new type of demon maybe once or twice but nothing that ever looked like this. These new demons were persistent beyond compare. To deter them Strat had even erected a wall over a mile long of stone. But not even two minutes later the Ravagers were back on their trail. They tried covering their track using earthen abilities, but the demons just ignored that and kept following without so much as a hesitation. Now they were galloping out right straight for the Giant Forest of Ancient oaks that within held the Ancient Elven City of Farthratrost Capitol of the Elven Lands and the seat of their ancient kings. Strat galloped to the front pushing ahead of everyone else and pulling even with Seth. Strat looked over towards him.

"Seth you see that Forest over there?" He asked. Seth eyes hadn't been focused on the road ahead at all. It was clear to Strat that his wounds were paining him. Seth looked up and his eyes widened.

"Holy... Those trees are huge!" Strat nodded. Indeed, they were.

"Head Straight for them the demons can't follow us inside!" Seth looked up at Strat confused the wind whipped wildly at Seth's hair.

"Why can't they follow us inside?" Strat wasted no time answering.

"That's where the Elven Capitol is. There's a barrier surround-ing the whole forest." Seth nodded and pulled on his reins with his uninjured left hand.

The Horses at this point gave them everything they had Strat had to be going at least sixty miles an hour. as were the rest of their group. But it didn't matter. The demons continued to gain ground. Strat and his group crested the hill that overlooked the valley in which the forest lay. Strat, now that he was closer could see the shimmering golden dome that covered the entire forest circling around the base still miles away was a patrol of eleven knights resplendent in their golden armor, elegant helms and spiked pauldrons even from where they were and traveling at the speed, they were Strat could make them out clearly. Strat looked back to make sure his companions were still heading in the right direction. Rylee and Mike were leading Aria and Michelle's horses, with them tied into the saddle. Seth was in front leading them and Jack and Travice were behind them. Bringing up the rear were Matt and John; both were desperately fending off attacks from the demons as they yet again closed the distance.

The knights who had been patrolling immediately spotted Strat and his group as they came barreling down the hill.

"Yangtosh Losphil" (Stop There!) The patrol yelled as it wheeled its horses to face Strat.

"Cartiligar Ownsiph," (Demon's behind us!) Strat yelled gesturing behind him as he spoke in Elvish. The lead Elven knight glanced behind Strat's group and noticed the demons nipping on their heels. The Elven leader seemed to look back and forth between the demons and Strat's group and for a split-second Strat was afraid they weren't going to let his group in. But then the elves began to sing. It was a silvery, beautiful voice that sang of protection and power. The Golden barrier expanded in Strat's direction and engulfed both him and his group passing harmlessly over them. But the demons behind him were rejected. Like hitting a steel wall, they slammed into the shield at full speed and several died on impact. the rest slid to a stop before they collided with the wall and began to stalk the wall back and forth like predators looking for any sign of weakness. After a few tense moments the demons turned and left running back in the direction they had come. Strat waited till they were out of sight before he let himself relax. Strat turned to the leader of the elven knights and clasped his hand in front of him while bowing his head. "Agates Tylis Secun." (Lord Tylis Greetings.) The lead Elf mirrored the movement.

"Agates Bannot Secun," (Lord Bannot Greetings.) (In Elvish) "What a welcome party for Lord Tylis to be personally patrolling the borders!" Strat said continuing with the pleasantries.

"Indeed, well times are tough within the Elven Lands, I still wouldn't expect the two great figures of the Academy to be chased by a mere pack of demons," The Eleven leader said sighing.

"Yeah, well as you said times are tough, speaking of time we have two injured comrades who need medical treatment immediately." Strat gestured behind him towards Aria and Michelle's horses. John, who was still in his boxers, got off his horse awkwardly in the back and began to get his armor on. Seth rode up beside Strat along with Jack. The minute Tylis Spotted Seth his eyes widened, and he bowed deeply in the saddle. Before Strat could warn him not to speak Tylis raised his clasped hands and spoke.

"Prince Sethias we have been waiting for your return!"

Chapter 15: Elven Capitol

Seth was at a complete loss for words.

"Um Strat who is Prince Sethias?" Seth asked cautiously. A collective gasp went up from those in the group. Strat who had one hand covering his face looked over at Seth clearly getting ready to tell him something. But before he could it all clicked with Seth. The reason his mom always said that his dad couldn't come home. Some of his earliest memories of a sharp eared man standing beside his bed, in a room made of wood.

"Great, the King is my dad, isn't he?" Seth said almost not even surprised by the fact. After the last year of discovering his mother was some kind of bad ass secret agent for God and then fighting an army and discovering demons and such one tends to stop being surprised even if he just found out that his father was the King of the

Elves. Strat didn't say anything to that he just nodded. He looked like he wanted to explain but Seth just shrugged it off.

"I know there was a reason, you were going to tell me, ex cetera, ex cetera. I get it, but what I would really like to know is why my mom didn't say anything." Strat reached up and scratched his head

"She was afraid that it would be too much of a shock for you."

"Too much for me really!?" Seth asked. "In the last year of my life alone I a. found out demons exist, b. was brought to a whole other world, and c. fought off and army of demons. What is her definition of too much? Strat nodded.

"That's fair but..."

"Guy's look," Rylee said. "It's great and all that you guys would like to have this conversation, but can we please do it later, we have two injured friends who need treating."

The elven leader reached up and removed his golden helm. Shoulder length blond hair fell out. He had and angular brow, but his skin looked incredibly smooth, without any wrinkles of age, his eyes were a pale green.

"The lady is right we need to get your friends back to the capitol first. This way, My Prince he said prompting Seth to follow the path in front of him.

The capitol was surprising in a lot of ways but in many ways, Seth knew what to expect. The buildings were all built into the trunks of the Great oaks each one was a wide a modern suburban home. If Seth had to guess he would have say they were about 2,000 square feet. Elves Roamed the roads, which were made of simple gravel. The canopy of trees made it so that great shafts of light pierced the tree illuminating the city below. In the shadowy places little balls of light danced around in the air giving those living there light. Seth watched as his Friends Aria and Michelle were rushed into a clinic just inside the city. He was worried for them, but he knew they had been through far worse. They would pull through. Just as he was deep in thought from behind a building came two kids probably around five or six years old, they were riding of what looked like a deer except it had six legs instead of two and was roughly the size of a horse. The creature glowed with a golden light, it's fur a silvery color. "What?" Seth began, in awe.

"While agents have the ability to create and manipulate matter with their light abilities, We Elves can create Living creatures with ours." Lord Tylis explained clearly amused with Seth's awe.

"Really!" Seth exclaimed. "That's amazing."

"It is, but there are limitations. For example We can't create anything too big unless we have the energy for it and if we are killed, all our creations die with us. Which is one of the reasons we value life above everything except The Lord." Seth nodded his understanding. As he noticed Strat had exited the clinic.

"The Doctors say they will be just fine but they need to rest for a few days so it looks like we will be here for a little bit. I hope that doesn't inconvenience you Lord Tylis?" Tylis shook his head. "Not at all I'll have your lodging arranged in the mean time I would like all of you to accompany me to go see the King I know he would very much like to meet his Son and I also assume there is another reason you all are here. You could talk to him directly about it. We'll leave the horses here. don't worry they'll be well looked after." Seth looked back at the group, everyone seemed to be staring at him to make a decision.

"Why are you all looking at me!? Seth asked.

"Well, they are your people," Mike said his usual quiet behavior gone in the excitement of visiting the Elven Capitol.

"And you are the prince," Matt said a tone of laughter hanging in his voice.

"Right, and we are going to meet your father, Jack said."

"No, you are all just lazy and don't want to have to think too much right!" Seth fumed.

"Right you are again," Travis said smiling. "My you are really good at this. My Prince." The sarcasm was so thick Seth could almost cut it with a knife.

"You guys are really not going to let this whole Prince thing go, are you?" Seth said sighing.

"Dang he's good," Rylee said, and Seth heard Strat snicker.

"Really guys we're supposed to all be grown-ups here some of you more so than others," Seth said throwing a look at Strat and Rylee. Rylee shrugged her shoulders.

"Being serious all the time is tiring, besides that's what we have Jack for am I right." Then all at once the tension the entire group had been feeling up until that point was dispersed as they all began to laugh. Seth saw Tylis shake his head with a confused look on his face.

"Human's," He said exasperated. Seth turned to him trying to suppress his laughter.

"Sorry, Lord Tylis please, Lead the way."

Chapter 16: Family

The Palace as it was called by the elves was a sight to see. It was built into the side of a Great white tree several thousands of square feet wide. With many tiered windows and by Seth estimate at least six floors. The glass was done in a fashion that the fourteen century Kings would be proud of and the impossibly thick roots scattered out in every direction. The leaves hanging from the tree were every color of the rainbow, and each was from a different type of tree.

"It's called the Tree of Origin or in Elvish it is pronounced as Elishiam," Tylis commented. Two of its great roots extended out from the tree in a semi-circle. and built into the roots were two sets of staircases that led up to two gigantic double iron doors. In between these two roots was a beautifully carved fountain made out of pure marble. It had the fierce likeness of angles carved into it. And not your cute baby looking kind but the true angels fierce warriors with eyes of lightning and wings of light. Which is why it was so impressively carved. How much skill does it take to carve life like lightning? Seth wondered. As he stared up at the iron double doors that were trimmed in golden patterns, he took a deep breath to prepare himself for what was about to happen. "What was his dad like," He wondered. "Will he even remember Seth, and how will he break the news about his mother. These questions kept whirling around in Seth's head as they were led up the steps to the big doors. Tylis put his hand lightly on the door and it began to open of it's own accord. Seth felt a hand on his shoulder he turned to see Strat looking at him concerned.

"You ready for this?" He asked.

Seth shrugged "As ready as I'll ever be, I suppose."

"Good! But I should warn you there is one more surprise in store for you in regard to your family, but I'll Let your father tell you." Seth shook his head.

"Of course, that's not the end of the secrets," He said. He looked back at Strat, but he was just smiling. Seth entered the big tree with everyone else and was completely taken aback. the colors inside were so vibrant. They were brought into a large circular room, Lining the room were twelve high backed thrones made of a pure white wood with red velvet cushioning. all these chairs sat facing the center of the room. and directly across from the entrance upon a raise dais was the thirteenth chair but this one was gold and had blue velvet seating. in each chair around the room sat an elf all young looking and even glowing with power. Up on the dais a man sat in the throne. He wore golden armor like that of the knights they had seen before, His long black hair was tied up in a bun and a regal crown of gold sat upon his head. The minute Seth's group entered Their eyes locked and Seth could feel the deep wisdom behind his golden eyes. wisdom born from living a very long time. Beside him stood a very pretty elf she was easily taller than Seth the same long black hair as the one sitting in the throne. She was tall and lithe she looked to be fast. From what Seth could tell she was eyeing Seth's group with suspicion. Seth turned back to the king as Lord Tylis and Strat stepped forward to announce their group.

"Your Majesty Stevos I'm sorry to interrupt your meeting with the honored elders, but we have visitors from the Lightforce Academy, very special visitors." The king waved it off.

"Think nothing of it Tylis." A smile broke out on his face as he stood and came forward arms open. He embraced Strat in a brotherly hug. "It's been too long old friend," He said Excitedly. Strat nodded in response.

"Indeed, it has been but not as long as it has been for you two, he said gesturing behind him to where Seth was standing. Stevos looked over at Seth a moment of confusion on his face. But then it cleared, and in a weak voice Seth heard his father say his name for the first time. "Seth? Is that you my son," He asked, the powerful and impossibly deep voice of a king he had been using before melted away as he rushed to hug Seth. Seth unsure of how to react did not move as he was embraced. He was unsure how he should feel. He vaguely heard Tylis announcing who he was.

"Announcing the return of Prince Sethias Son of Lord Stevos and Katie Malcovitch." A collective gasp filled the air as the elders reacted in shock. Seth's father pulled back and seemed to study Seth's face.

"You remind me of your mother," he said. Then another confused look crossed over his face, and he looked behind Seth as if he was searching for someone. "Speaking of which where is your mother? I'm sure she would've like to come herself." When Seth didn't answer Strat spoke up.

"Actually, Stevos that's why we've come. We have a lot to talk about." Stevos's eyes narrowed and he stepped back.

"What's..." He never got to finish because as before Seth could react, he had been pushed out of the way and the girl who was standing beside him a moment ago pushed him out of the way and embraced Seth. Seth's friends gasped.

The pretty elf pulled back and eyed Seth with a Mischievous grin. "So, you are the Older brother my father has told me so much about."

Seth blinked several times before his brain began to process what had just been said.

"Sis..ter? I... Have a sister!" Seth was dumbfounded but Strat who was next to him began to bust out laughing.

"Dad you didn't tell me that my brother was this good look-ing." The girl said.

"Elisha now is not the time, perhaps we should talk about this later, I sense we have an issue that brings your brother and his friends to our door." Seth's dad said clearly trying to change the topic. The

Elders around the room seemed to be smiling as if they found this girls breach of decorum to be refreshing. Seth tried to pull himself together. He took a deep breath and began to explain but he couldn't figure out how to address his dad.

"S... Sir. I mean your majesty, I... mean..."

"Just call me Stevos or Father. It wouldn't do for my own son to have to be so formal with me." Seth took a deep breath.

"F... Father," He managed. It felt weird coming from his mouth, so he settled for using the other one.

"Stevos, we came to find you because Katie, my mother, was captured by demons two day's ago." Seth said.

Chapter 17: Place of Hiding

"What do you mean she was captured!" Stevos said. His voice now carried a dangerous tone in his voice that was in complete contrast to his earlier friendly attitude. It was so intense that it made Seth take an involuntary step back. Strat stepped forward.

"She was taken by demons when the academy was attacked by demon dragons." Stevos's eyes widened.

"Dragons, I thought the dragons left this world long ago," He said. Strat nodded.

"Yeah, me too I remember we were both there when they flew off, but these dragons are nothing like them, these are artificially made." Seth couldn't follow what they were saying anymore, it was like both of them had stopped trying to include anyone else into their conversation.

"artificially made? How?"

"I'm afraid it's Zach's doing," Strat said. Stevos raised an eyebrow.

"Mr. Warstroff? I knew I had a bad feeling about him when you first introduced him to me." Stevos began to pace back and forth in the throne room. To Seth he looked like he was deep in thought, until one of the elders spoke up.

"Well, why was she taken?" A thirteen-year-old looking elder said. His white hair at least gave others the impression that he was an elder, if you did not look to closely at his face.

"Because she knows the location of the Air Gem," Seth replied. Stevos did not reply at first, but as Seth had guessed Seth only had to say that and Stevos had already guessed why they were there.

"You are here for it's location correct?" He asked. Seth stepped forward. Yes, it's the only way we can find the air gem before they manage to get my mother to divulge the information." Stevos turned

to Seth concern in his eyes.

"Are you not worried about your mother?" Seth pushed down

the rush of complicated emotions. He had a mission to complete.

"Are you not concerned they will kill her."

"Of course, I'm worried!" Seth exclaimed a little louder than

he had meant to. He took a deep breath to calm himself.

"Look Stevos," Strat interrupted. "It's not a matter of if they

get her to talk it's a matter of when. You know as well as I do that

Katie is as tough as nails but me and you also know how ruthless

the demons are and how effective their torture techniques are.

They will get her to talk and once she is of no more use to them

then they will kill her. But before then they will not kill her. They

need her after all. But the fact that they are searching for the air

gem means they are likely going to the same places we are which

will mean we will have a chance to rescue her, but we need the location first." Stevos seemed to take this into the account, as he thought.

"Bring me a map!" He ordered. Within minutes guards rushed in a large round table and then another guard came in with a rolled-up map under his arm. They quickly set up the table and brought in the map and laid it across the table. Seth could see the academy lands in the south and the Minoan Plains to the north of the Academy lands and even further to the north was a gigantic mountain range that ran the entire width of the continent it was this place that Stevos pointed at. "The Durante Mounts this was the place she told me. In the ancient floating fortress of Aralu that sits above them."

"Really Katie, "Strat sighed. Seth understood what he meant. It had to be in the furthest possible region from them and in a "floating fortress," at that.

"Really," Rylee said. "She couldn't have hidden it anywhere closer, like I don't know here in the elven lands or better yet back at the Academy."

"Isn't that Dwarven territory," John asked.

"Yes, it is but that's the easy part," Stevos said.

"The hard part is that the only way to access the city is through a portal that's located in a very remote part of the Dwarven Mounts a small dwarven settlement by the name of Ragarstea. So, you'll need to acquire a guide from one of the dwarven settlements on the outskirts of the mounts." Strat tapped the map deep in thought.

"It's a little out of the way but I think I know who we can get for a guide.

"How far out of the way are we talking?" Jack asked from beside Seth. Seth hadn't even known that Jack was standing there.

Strat shook his head. "I know what you're thinking Jack but no it's not that. It is not even a day out of our way. But it won't matter because according to the Healers it is going to take at least two days for Aria and Michelle to recover enough to travel so we will be here for at least that long." Jack opened his mouth to protest but Strat spoke first.

"I know time of the essence but there are things we can't rush. we need to be properly prepared and for that we will need Both miss Aria and Miss Michelle." Jack still looked like he wanted to say something but in the end he just nodded. "Besides," Strat said in a tone that immediately gave Seth a sinking feeling that made him feel as if he might not enjoy his time at the elven capitol as much. "This will give me more time to continue training young Seth here."

Chapter 18: Elemental Armor

After the meeting adjourned Seth's father directed a guardsman to show them to the guest rooms. Seth turned to go as well but he felt a hand tug at his cloak. He turned to find his sister looking at him.

"What is it," Seth said saying it harsher than he meant to. She visibly flinched at the bite in his voice.

"Don't you want to stay and talk?" she asked. "I've been waiting to meet you for well... forever and now that you're here you just want to ignore me?" Seth turned and patted her on her shoulder armor.

"It's not as if I want to ignore you, but you have got to give me time to register all this. I did not even know you existed till today, or that my father was the King of an entire race! It's ... It's just that it's going to take me some time to adjust." She looked like she wanted to say something, but Seth turned and began walking away.

Seth exited the Castle and without waiting for anyone else he wandered off his heart in turmoil. He was so deep in thought in fact that he didn't even pay attention to where he was going. He just wandered passing by several elves and townspeople who all regarded him with curiosity as he passed by. No doubt wondering what a human was doing wondering their city. Seth continued to wonder until he found himself on the outskirts of the city staring up at an impossibly large oak tree. With not many elves around here Seth was immediately alerted to the sound of footsteps behind him. When he turned to look, he discovered it was Rylee who had followed him. Seth turned his back on her without saying a word, not sure what to say. It was then that Rylee did something completely unexpected. Although Seth heard her approaching, he could only gasp when he felt her wrap her arms around him and give him a hug.

"You know..." She said awkwardly. "You aren't alone. You have people you can talk to, and although I don't know what's going on in that head of yours, we... I am always here to listen." Seth slightly turned to look at her. Her auburn eyes matching her hair met his at the same time. Seth saw her blush a deep scarlet and quickly let go of him stepping back. Seth turned to face her.

"Thank you for caring Rylee it means a lot to me." Still blushing Rylee only nodded.

"Even when you are a hundred years old a girl is still a girl," a voice said. Seth turned to it and saw his dad walking toward them. "But she's not wrong. I know circumstances have kept us apart until now but now that I have the chance, I would like to get to know my son." Seth said nothing not sure what to say back to that. "However, that isn't why I came." Seth raised an eyebrow in question.

"Strat said he was looking for you to start your training."

Seth groaned, "Already, he really is a slave driver."

Rylee laughed "Yeah well you've only scratched the surface with most of your powers, and if anyone can get you ready before we set out day after tomorrow its Stratos." Seth thought for a moment and began to grin.

"Well, then we shouldn't keep him waiting."

…

Seth stood facing Strat on an open field commonly used for training. Nearby his Father, the King, stood by observing silently.

"Seth your powers and abilities have always been outstanding," Strat began to lecture. "But you have only scratched the surface."

"So, I have been told," Seth said while briefly glancing over to where Rylee was standing.

"Yes, well as you've discovered there are many applications to our abilities. such as controlling more precise and accurate attacks. But..." Strat paused as if to let the word hang in the air for dramatic effect. "There are other applications such as hand to hand combat and body enhancement."

Seth blinked, "Hand to hand combat and Body enhancement? Wait a moment I thought all the sword training was the hand to hand?" Strat laughed; it was a refreshing act because Seth rarely saw Strat laugh. "No, that was the weapon training. You can think of that as phase one of this training. Next, I am going to show you how to feel the energy God gave you and infuse both your body and weapon with this energy to increase both your body's physical performance and its movement speed. For example." As Strat said this Seth felt and immense pressure in his ears. His ears popped as the air pressure around Strat dropped. Seth found himself unable to move an inch as pressure seemed to push Seth into the ground. "This, is air pressure, a skill you can use to slow down or in most cases even immobilize your opponents in close proximity to yourself. Very effective in close combat. But you have already learned much about controlling the element of air. So, let's use an element you have yet to materialize or utilize. Which element have you used the least?"

Seth thought for a moment. "Lightning, that's definitely the element I've used the least besides darkness. Which I don't even know how to manifest yet." Strat seemed to pause while thinking.

"Lightning huh, yeah I can do something with that. As he said this, he assumed a wide stance and briefly closed his eyes to focus. Seth was wondering what he was doing, and as it turned out he wouldn't have to wait long. As Seth watched electricity began to spark and flicker across Strat's body with an audible pop. Seth felt his hair stand on end as ozone charged the air around them. Seth blinked and felt a gasp escape from him. The reason for this gasp was that now Strat was covered in a thin almost imperceptible layer of lighting. Strat's curly hair now stood on end and every part of his body seemed like it was vibrating. Energy rolled off Strat in waves. Everyone present and watching seemed to stop and gawk at the blue and white electricity sparking and popping around Strat. Even Seth's dad had a look of utter surprise upon his face. When he spoke, his voice seemed to be distorted like there was a delay between when he spoke and when the sound actually came out.

"I call this Elemental armor," Strat's distorted voice said. "It's used to enhance both your speed..." Seth blinked and Strat was no longer in front of him. He felt a subtle tap on his shoulder, and he turned around to find Strat standing behind him energy crackling around him.

Seth's eyes widened in surprise as he threw himself backward out of Strat's range. It was an involuntary action; one Seth's body took when it sensed a presence behind him. He heard Strat's laughter.

"You always did have impressive reflexes. But speed isn't this energy's only use. It can also increase your Power!" With these last words Strat walked over to a rather thick tree nearby an extended his hand toward it palm facing outward as he lightly touched the tree's trunk. The Effect was almost immediate, A hole the size of a basket-ball was instantly opened in the tree's trunk. Seth felt his eyes widen slightly in wonder. Most intermediate agents know this skill and can manipulate their element to even greater heights with this ability. But Since we are heading into what is most likely going to be a trap, I thought I should teach you this technique. Are you ready to begin?" Elemental Armor holy crap, Seth thought. If I had known about this earlier the number of ways, I could've used it is unimaginable. The idea of being able to infuse his power with his body and weapon was such a cool idea it made Seth's blood boil in anticipation. He secretly began thinking of other ways his powers could be used. But outwardly Seth just nodded enthusiastically. Strat nodded to himself before the lightning flickering around him stopped all at once. Strat raised his hand palm facing the sky. and Lightning began to flicker around it.

"What you need to do first is manifest lightning in the palm of your hand. This shouldn't be a problem for you," Strat said as he then manipulated the lightning into his palm. "Next instead of releasing it like you normally would, you need to imagine drawing the power into your body." Strat closed his eyes to demonstrate this.

"You need to feel the energy throughout every part of your body. Feel it flow to every part of your body. Feel it surge and understand it was God who bestowed this amazing power upon you." Strat's blue lightning armor reignited as sparks flew from every part of his body.

Seth closed his eyes and reached out his right-hand palm up exactly as Strat had done. He pictured lightning appearing above his palm. He felt the familiar energy drain as he began hearing the popping of sparks. This indicated that he had succeeded. However, he did not open his eyes instead he pictured that power flowing through his hand to the rest of his body.

Seth felt the normal pull on his energy reserve increase nearly tenfold. But everything else seemed to increase. His hearing, and his sight increased. He was suddenly hearing things he couldn't hear previously. And seeing farther than he could before. The intake of new information caused him to stumble backward losing focus. His power dissipated.

"Seth!" Seth heard Stevos exclaim. Seth lost his footing and almost fell before he felt a hand grab him arm steadying him. Seth glanced behind him to see Strat holding him up. Strat was smiling, a mischievous look in his eye.

"You knew that was going to happen, didn't you?" Seth asked his vision still swimming. Strat nodded his smile only growing.

"The intake of new information is too much for anyone on their first time. Did you feel the energy drain?" Seth nodded. The drain on his energy had been twice that of when he used his normal abilities. But even with that amount of energy being taken from him he still had plenty to spare. But he had to admit, at the most he could probably keep the Elemental armor going for about an hour, but first, he had to get past this feedback. Strat helped Seth to his feet, and He looked Seth up and down. "Do you think you can try again." Seth's excitement soared. It had been almost a year and a half since he had first discovered his powers. and He was more excited now than he had been then. The possibilities of this new power were endless, and Seth couldn't wait to learn more. Seth saw Strat notice his smile, and in response he also was grinning madly. "Alright then, Let's get started."

Chapter 19: The Threat

After two days of rigorous training with Strat, Seth had managed to hold the Lightning Elemental Armor for about half an hour, and that was all. Strat said that the outcome had been the best that could be expected within the time that they had been given, but Seth couldn't shake his sense of disappointment that he couldn't achieve more during this time. During these two days Seth had chosen not to speak with his family much. It was not that he hated his new family or that he was angry with them. He simply found it awkward to talk with them. How do you start a conversation with a person you haven't spoken with in almost 17 years? "Hey how has the last 17 years been?" No Seth knew it would take more than two or three days for this awkwardness to subside. Seth and the rest of his friends were standing near the edge of the barrier. Seth's dad and his sister had come to see them off. Aria and Michelle had made a complete recovery under the careful watch of the elves. Both wore fresh clothes under their newly polished armor. The brown cloaks that their entire group wore over their armor had been freshly washed.

Stevos

"I wish you could stay longer," Stevos said his eyes clearly lingering on Seth. Seth averted his eyes unsure of what to say.

"As do I," Strat said clasping Stevos's arm and pulling him into a hug.

"The little girl that came with you will be safe with use for the remainder of your journey."

"I appreciate your help with that," Strat said sincerely.

"It's not a problem, she is welcome to stay with my people as long as she wishes. I just wish she had some family for her. But nevertheless, we will treat her as if she is one of our own," Stevos said.

Strat mounted his horse and turning around he led the way through the barrier.

The King of the Elves kept his eyes on his son as he watched his son mount his horse and leave his city on his way to save the world.

"Do you think we will see him again," His daughter Elisha asked as she watched the retreating back of her older brother." Stevos did not even need to think about it.

"Of course, we will, he is our family after all," he answered. But Elisha frowned her golden eyes showing the uncertainty she was feeling.

"Are you sure? He didn't seem to be thrilled to meet us." Stevos couldn't help but sigh. He also had been very worried about how Seth seemed to keep them at arm's length while he had been staying with them.

"Elisha we can't judge your brother by normal standards. It is not his fault that he had no contact with us for all those years. It can't be easy trying to connect with a family that you didn't know you had." His daughter shifted uncomfortably hopping from one foot to the other.

"Well why do you think mom never told him about us?" Once again Stevos was uncertain how to reply.

"That's a very good question daughter, that's a very good question.

Katie

Katie opened her eyes to see thick steel bars that had been imbued with the power of shadows. This was of course to dampen or even cancel out her abilities. They had been on the move for a few days now. they kept her cage covered so that she could not tell where they were going. From the feel of the terrain over the last day or so Katie would have to say that they had entered the mountains. How they were transporting her was beyond her knowledge because she was locked in a cage that was capped on two ends by a slab of concrete. But they were indeed moving that much she could tell. However, she had no idea where she was being taken and that made her anxious. If she knew where they were taking her, she could find a way to facilitate and escape. she could leave clues for example, but since she had been kept completely in the dark there was no way. She had only tried a forceful escape once and well... Katie coughed as the pain of her broken ribs became apparent. A souvenir of her doomed attempt at an escape a few days ago.

Katie was careful to try and pick-up clues as to where they were going by picking up the chatter of the demons. Demons as a rule didn't usually speak much. As a matter of fact, most of them didn't even have the intelligence required to be able to even form a coherent sentence. It probably made them easier to control. But there were some demons who possessed enough intelligence to talk and act on their own. However, these were mostly the High-ranking demons and those in a position of power. Katie would listen to every bit of conversation she heard no matter how remote or unrelated. She also paid close attention to the demon's behavior as they traveled. So, she was immediately aware of the guard's shift in pace. They were excited and anxious, which led Katie to believe they were about to arrive at their destination. Wherever that was. This was soon confirmed as the terrain changed yet again. now they were going down at a very steep pace. Wherever they were going it was clearly underground. It did not take a mastermind to figure that out. Katie stayed quiet; she had done her best to remain strong throughout this ordeal. She had kept her head cool, kept herself under control and calm. But now, realizing that she was near her destination made her confront the thought that she might not make it back from this one, and that scared her, more than she was willing to admit. Of course, she wanted to go to heaven and see the friends and family she'd lost, but she also had a pretty good reason to stay and it was her son. By, now if her plan had worked out right, he would have met his father and his sister.

"Was he going to hate her for not telling him about them? All these thoughts came swirling into her head causing her to quickly be overwhelmed emotionally. Three days of keeping it together and she just couldn't anymore. When the first of the tears began to trickle down her face she tried to hold them back, she didn't want to cry in front of her enemy. However, as they continued unabated by her efforts in the slightest, she stopped fighting them and just let them fall. The tears came like an unstoppable waterfall. And soon she was hopelessly sobbing. She tried to tell herself that there was no shame in crying. In the situation she was in most women would have broken down before the demons had even laid a hand on them. But she wasn't just any woman. She was the Chief Commander of the Lightforce she had a fearless reputation to uphold.

"Get a hold of yourself Katie," Katie mumbled to herself. "You will get out of this and make it home to Seth." Mustering her courage, Katie reached up and wiped the tears from her eyes determined to not show any fear in the face of whatever happened next. Above all she had to remember that God was with her. No matter where she was or how deep in enemy lines, they took her, they could never take her away from God. Simply knowing that Katie sighed in relief. She wasn't alone, no she was never alone, because God was with her. And, whether or not she made it out of here wouldn't change that fact that God had her back. Katie raised her eyes up towards the concrete slab that served as her ceiling.

"God, I hope you've got a plan for this one, you've gotten me through some pretty tough spots in the past, so I ask that we get through one more." Saying that Katie took a deep breath to steel herself for what was to come.

...

They brought her deeper and deeper underground, for hours it seemed they travelled onwards. But Katie could see none of it. The Air warmed and then it became uncomfortably hot. A putrid smell began to permeate the air, Sulfur! They were under a volcano, But Katie didn't think the continent of Elementia had any active volcanoes. Further on they travelled until at last they halted. Katie pressed herself to the bar trying to listen to anything being said. The voice she heard sent shivers rolling down her back. She had heard this voice plenty of times before and knew who this voice belonged to.

"Open it up let her out I want to see the great face of the Chief Commander!" Suddenly the ground fell out beneath Katie as she fell roughly onto a rocky floor. A brief cry escaped from her lips as she felt her broken ribs flare up in pain. But she tried to quickly get her Barings. Looking around she quickly realized that they were in a massive cavern, and saying it was massive was an understatement. The cavern was easily several miles wide and it stretched so far that Katie couldn't see where it ended in the gloom. The floor of the cavern also seemed to be shrouded in a shadowy fog, and a thick one at that. Suddenly the voice spoke again this time right next to her.

"How was the trip Commander I assume it was pleasant." Katie turned to the owner of the voice. He was about six feet tall, so he towered over her. He was clad in the black spiky plate armor of the demons except for one crucial thing he wasn't a demon. his skin was a pale milky white, his angular face stared down at hers with his Icy cold blue eyes. Atop his head sat a mop of brown hair that seemed unruly. A playful smirk was plastered on his face, that reminded Katie of the days she used to watch this man when he was a kid. Before he had been chosen as one of the elementists and before he had betrayed the Lightforce. Before he had turned. Zachery Warstroff! Apprentice of Stratos, Now called the Scourge of Light! Katie pursed her lips to speak but then firmly shut her mouth, she would not let this scum have the honor of even talking with her. Warstroff smiled at her attempt to spurn him.

"Not talking huh. That's fine I don't need you to talk I just need you to listen. and although we had originally kidnapped you to have you reveal to us the location of the Air Elemental gem, that is no longer necessary. So, Lord Reaper has asked me to entrust you with a message before letting you go!"

This got a reaction out of Katie despite herself.

"You're going to just let me go, you're not going to kill me." Zach looked at her mocking surprise.

"Kill you! No no no, why would I do that when I can see you run home in despair." The smile on his face sickened Katie.

"How do I know you aren't lying?" Katie asked not daring to get her hopes up. These were demons she had to remind herself. There was no way they were going to let her go that easily. They wanted something out of this.

"You don't know," Zach simply replied. "But first let me go ahead and give you the message before you decide. You might decide you want to die right here instead of waiting."

"Waiting for what?" Katie asked.

"For the war," Zach replied.

"What war?"

"This one!" Zach exclaimed motioning out toward the open cavern with his hand. Katie followed his motion, and she felt her face freeze. Fear had gripped her. Even knowing God was with her she was only human, and humans would feel fear in the face of what she was seeing. Down in the cavern the shadowy fog had cleared up to reveal a massive army of demons preparing for war. As Katie's eyes followed their movements, she felt a chill in her blood. Never in her hundred years of life had she ever seen so many demons in one place. Not even in the previous war with Reaper had there been this many. They stretched into the gloom of the cavern. There had to be millions if not billions of demons down there covering the ground like a thick black carpet. But something was off about them, upon closer inspection, Katie discovered that some of the demon's down there were differ- ent from any demons she had fought before.

There were small stocky demons that wielded giant glowing war hammers, and sleek shadowy demons that moved extremely fast. There were demons riding on horseback, and still other demons in thick hooded robes. Though the last kind was rare. Katie could also make out the silhouette of several dark dragons in the far back.

"Katie this is my lord's formal Declaration of War against the Academies. You are to go back to the Academies and prepare what resistance you can offer." Katie frowned.

"Why?" she asked. Zach raised an eyebrow mockingly.

"why are we doing this? Well, I suppose I could tell you it's for some righteous cause but we both know that it would be a lie. But if I had to choose a reason." Zach smiled "It's because it's fun!" Zach spread his arms out to either side like he had just made grand statement.

"No, I don't care what sick reason you have for doing this I just want to know why you are bothering with a formal declaration, wouldn't it have been easier to just launch a surprise attack?" Zach's smile faded.

"I thought so too but unfortunately I'm not the boss around here. But I look at it this way. Now, you won't have any excuses when you lose."

"We won't lose to you," Katie said calmly, fully in her heart she believed it too. She had been in a war once before if she could fight then she could fight now.

"Yeah, well let's agree to disagree," Zach replied. "Now the guards will take you away and let you go at an undisclosed location. Can't have you knowing where are base is." Katie took a deep breath, pushing her fear deep down. War had been declared and the Academies had to be ready, she had work to do. Two demons stepped forward with a black hood they were going to put over her head. Zach turned and began to walk away.

"Oh, and by the way I'm off to meet that darling son of your and some old friends, they do not have the same guarantee that they will return. So, I look forward to what kind of funeral you will arrange," he told her like it was an afterthought. But it struck Katie to the core. And she realized that Zach knew where her son was going. But before she could say anything, she felt a sharp pain in the base of her skull and her consciousness faded.

Chapter 20: Oliver The Dwarf

Seth

Seth and his friends had been traveling for about a day now and the air had become crisp and cool. The ground had slowly begun to rise at a steady pace as the Mighty Dwarf Mounts loomed ahead casting a shadow on the land at their base. At the base of one of the mountains sat a tiny walled village made of stone that sat peacefully beside a river. This is where they were headed. The Dwarven town Burdenfawlk. The small town didn't look like much it had a simple stone wall and stone building that had clay shingled roofs. For as small as the city was Seth was surprised to find that there were actually quite a few hunters and trappers here. They entered the city after explaining to the dwarven guard at the gate that they had come seeking a guide to the mountain village.

After telling the guard who they were looking for they were directed to a low building that sat on the outskirts of the town. As they approached Seth noticed several tanning racks with fresh hides drying on them outside. The low stone house had a thatched ceiling instead of the shingled roofs they'd seen causing it to stand out. From a chimney a plume of black smoke billowed out. A short grey horse was tied to a post outside. Strat motioned for Seth and the others to stay back and then he slowly trotted up to the front of the house acting as casual as can be.

Staying on his horse Seth watched as Strat made a fist and slapped it across his chest horizontally and shouted.

"Hail! Dwarfen Oliver!" almost immediately a call came in reply from the small house.

"Hail! Human Stratos!" A small dwarf opened his door. He wasn't as broad shouldered as Barbratoss. And his body wasn't as wide but he had a thick brown beard upon his face that hid his mouth so Seth couldn't tell whether he was happy to see them or not. On top of his head sat a head of curly brown hair. He was wearing a set of steel plated armor that was exquisitely made. carved into the armor was a language Seth didn't understand. The Dwarven language! Seth realized quickly that this dwarf didn't belong in this town of hunters. Not only was he wearing the heavy plate armor of the dwarves but strapped to his back were two one handed axes. These axes were about two feet long with wide blades made out of a blue metal that seemed to pulsate in the light. The long wooden handles were wrapped in leather while the blade was traced in gold. They gave off a dazzling aura that Seth realized made it very hard to look away from them. Seth shook his head trying to free himself from the trance he was in.

"So how have you been old friend?" Strat asked as he dismounted his horse. The dwarf named Oliver maintained his neutral expression.

"Cut the crap," He said indifferently. "I know why you are here Barbratoss's message reached me yesterday and I am already ready to go so we shouldn't waste any time.

"Wait Barbratoss contacted you?" Strat asked stunned. The dwarf didn't answer as he mounted his small grey horse.

"Yeah, he sent a letter explaining the situation and that you would probably come for my help."

Strat sighed as he remounted his horse. "As expected of Barbratoss his insight is as impeccable as always."

"We'll talk on the way we have a long climb ahead of us." Without so much as introductions Oliver turned his horse and began to trot away through the city but he didn't make it far before he stiffened. Seth sensed it at that moment as well.

"How'd they get into the city?" The dwarf asked almost to himself as he pulled one of his hand axes out of its shoulder sheathe. Seth nudged his horse to the front of the group as he pulled Sonfang, flashes of light and the sound of ringing steel indicated that the rest of his friends also drew weapons. Seth made way as Strat and jack moved their horses beside his.

"It's the new type," Jack muttered. When Oliver looked at him for explanation it was actually Strat who provided it. Seth kept his eyes on the road in front of him. The sleek figures of the shadow hunter demons were keeping to the shadows of the town.

"They're not attacking at least," Seth said as he observed them.

"They are probably waiting for us to leave the city," Mike said speaking up.

"Yeah, that makes the most sense, they'd be stupid to attack us in this dwarven city. There are guards all over the place," Matt said a thoughtful but firm expression on his face.

"So, once we get out of the city we make a break for it," John said loading his bizarre gun with what looked like seeds.

"Sounds good to me," Aria said.

"But what if they follow us?" Rylee asked eyeing Strat.

"Oh, that's easy," The dwarf said his thick beard parting into a grin. "We fight!"

Chapter 21: Ambush

Stratos

It didn't take the demons long to catch up with their group. The demons moved swiftly running far faster than normal demons could. They could've overtaken them if they wanted, but for some reason they were staying just behind them occasionally firing bolts of darkness at the group. Something about this didn't sit right with Strat. Shouldn't the demons be trying to keep them away from the portal? So, why did it seem like they were being herded in the direction of the portal it was almost like they wanted them to go there... Strat immediately stopped his horse in the middle of the path.

"What are you doing Strat?" Jack called swinging his horse to a stop as well. But everyone could sense that something was off, Strat sensed something. Even Oliver who had just joined the group knew to trust Strat's instincts.

"It's a trap!?" Strat exclaimed openly showing alarm on his face. "And a clever one at that." Jack's eyebrows narrowed "A trap how do you figure?" Jack asked, pulling the hood of his brown cloak down to scan the surroundings.

Strat jumped off his horse and took up a position of cover. "I'll explain it, but first let's get rid of our pursuers. Seth quickly followed raising his own earth shield in the path and taking cover behind it. The others follow just in time for bolts of darkness to start exploding around them. Strat, however, knew that they didn't have time for a long-drawn-out fight. So, Strat decided to release the power he normally concealed, at least a little bit of it. Quickly stomping on the ground Strat imagined the earth splitting open and swallowing the demons into its depths. Strat reached out to the demon's positions using the earth to sense where they were. The effects were immediate. The ground shook as a crack formed at the feet of each demon, quickly widening into a crevice that swallowed them whole before they could react. The fight was over as soon as it began.

"Strat what was that?" a voice asked from behind Strat. Strat turned around to find John with an apprehensive look on his face. Through his power over nature, he could probably sense what Strat had done, and since he had never actually seen Strat in action before he seemed to be quite surprised by his strength.

Strat shrugged," We are out of time if we want to get through that portal. Because if waiting for us at that portal is who I think it is, we are in for a world of hurt. It was now that Jack seemed to catch on to Strat's line of thinking.

"You think Zach is waiting for us at the portal huh?" Strat simply nodded without looking at him.

"What makes you think that?" Travis asked a skeptical look on his face. Strat shrugged, because we have to assume, he already knows we are coming, and this is the move I would take if I were in his position. Strat had an intense look on his face. Strat stroked his chin as he tried to think of a way out of the trap, they had found themselves in. Zach had made it to where there was only one move, he could possibly make. Standing up Strat looked to his friends especially Seth, who had an uncertain look on his face.

"There is no way around it," Strat said with a sigh. He had made peace with what he had to do.

"What is that look for?" Seth asked becoming uncomfortable under Strat's gaze. Strat heard a gasp and turned to see Matt his eyes wide with shock a look of understanding dawning on his face, and then his facial expression hardened as he began to stare Strat down. Strat immediately realized that Matt had figured out what he was planning.

"No Stratos, I won't let you, you are too important."

"It's the only way," Strat replied calmly. "Only I have the power necessary to hold him back for any significant amount of time. Besides it's the reason I came with you guys." After this realization dawned in the eyes of each of his friends as they understood his intentions.

"Strat no!" Seth exclaimed and Strat felt his heart ache. The last thing he wanted to do was leave these amazing people he'd gotten to know so well. But there wasn't any other option if they wished to get the Gem before anyone else.

Strat held up his hand to stall any further complaints before he looked his companions in the eyes one at a time.

"This is what must be done. Besides, I do not know What Zach has learned since I last saw him but there is a lot of you who know how powerful I am. There was no boast in his words. Because he didn't need to. It was an undeniable fact that Strat was one of if not the most powerful agent in the Lightforce Academies. These words seemed to quell their objections for the moment, but Strat could tell that Rylee and Matt still wanted to argue. Strat's eyes glanced to the side to where Jack was standing. Jack was without a doubt Strat's closest friend. Although Jack didn't speak much or interact with individuals, Strat and him had been through countless life and death battles together. They knew each other extremely well. But Jack said nothing, he simply looked up towards the mountain. Oliver who had been quite during this time cleared his throat.

"Can you all please do the sappy thing later we have a mission to complete." With this there was no more conversation. Strat turned to the group and explained then plan.

"I'm going to directly confront Zach, meanwhile it will be your guys jobs to get through the portal by any means necessary. That's the plan."

"Alright Oliver would you lead them on ahead. I need to have a word with Jack. We'll catch up with you." Everyone stared at him with curiosity, but they followed Oliver and once again started up the mountain. Strat waited until the group was out of sight before he turned to Jack.

"My friend how many tough spots have me and you found ourselves in over the years?" Strat was sure if he didn't try to convince Jack right here there would be no way that Jack would leave him.

Jack shrugged his eyes seemed trained on the spot up ahead where the rest of their friends had disappeared.

"So then do you really think I'll die here. I won't let Zach beat me."

"That's not what I'm worried about," Jack said in a low tone. Strat was puzzled.

"Then, what are you worried about?" Jack sighed and turned his green eyes on Strat.

"Strat, I'm worried that you won't be able to do what it takes to end this." Strat frowned immediately understanding what Jack meant. Zach had been Strat's pupil and instead of hate Strat felt a great sadness for Zach. So what jack was worried about was that Strat would let his guard down and attempt to persuade Zach. That could prove fatal if the other one was only out to kill you. Still Strat shook his head.

"Jack if you are going to ask me not to appeal to him, I'm going to tell you you're wasting your time. We are followers of God; Blind hate is not something that should be inherent to us. I will talk to him, but I'm not stupid Jack I can promise you I won't die from this." Strat turned away from Jack and began walking up the hill behind him in a soft voice he heard Jack say.

"I hope not my friend."

Chapter 22: Confrontation

Seth

It didn't take long for Strat and Jack to catch up with the rest of them, But Seth still was curious what the two said to each other. Seth wasn't really worried about Strat dying but he was concerned. He had never met this Zach before but from what everyone was saying he seemed like a real piece of work. Still as the day progressed Seth and his friends moved forward in silence. The only time there was any sort of conversation was when they stopped for a rest before continuing on. The air became even colder and the winds picked up. Before Seth knew it instead of lush grass snow could be seen everywhere. The trees became fewer and the path they were on narrowed until at times Seth could no longer see it. However, Oliver never seemed lost he would always lead them up the winding path without so much as a pause to check where he was going. To Seth it seemed like Oliver had taken this path many times before and knew every part by heart. If this was the case, then it would make since why Strat would choose him to be their guide.

As the air thinned the amount of breaks, they had to take increased as their bodies tried to overcome the difference in air quality. But it only took them about two hours to reach the outskirts of the village where the portal. When they were about half a mile still from the village according to Oliver, Oliver held up his hand quickly. He turned his head to the side as if he was listening intently for something. Seth closed his eyes and tried to sense something through the earth. But he couldn't feel anything. Seth opened his eyes and looked towards Oliver wondering if the dwarf was hearing things.

Then he heard it to, the thumping sound of a steady wing beat. It was clear and repetitive, a smooth rhythm. Soon, it was followed by another set of flapping, then another, and another.

"Quick into the brush!" Strat exclaimed as they scrambled for cover. Seth dove behind an outcropping of rocks just as an entire flock of dragons flew overhead. The wind from their wings shook the mountain as they flew overhead. The dragons were exactly as Seth remembered them. Midnight black scale and blood red spikes mad up their natural armor, but what really sent a chill down Seth's spine every time he saw one of these monstrosities was the blood red eyes. They seemed, so lifeless and murderous, like the only thing they cared for was how many they could kill. Seth crouched down trying to make himself smaller as he tried to estimate the number of dragons in the flock, but he lost count at forty two.

It seemed like it took forever but eventually the shadow dragons disappeared from sight and Seth and his friends began to relax.

"Damn I hate those things," Travis said and there were a lot of chorusing agreements from the group.

"Well," Strat started. "We are close enough to the village that I can make my way from here i want all of you guys to follow Oliver and why I'm distracting Zach try to sneak through the portal."

No one tried arguing, mostly because they knew it was point-less but also because they knew it had to be done. Seth stood and before Strat could protest Seth pulled him into a hug. Seth wasn't sure why he did it and he wasn't particularly emotional he just felt that if Strat didn't come back Seth would regret not saying goodbye in some form. Strat seemed shocked as he didn't react right away, he simply stood there. Seth quickly let go, not trying to make Strat feel awkward and stepped back smiling.

"You got this master Strat," Aria called.

"You can do it," Matt said.

"Show him who's boss!" Mike shouted.

"Come back Safe," Rylee said with a smile.

"Don't die," Michelle said stiffly.

"Teach him a lesson," John said in his deep voice.

Seth couldn't believe the support everyone was showing for Strat. It was more than just some encouragement everyone there truly believed that Strat would be just fine. It was a moment Seth knew would stick with him for the rest of his life. And it was also a moment Seth silently gave thanks to God that he had been able to make such good friends. Seth could tell that Strat was overwhelmed because he gave everyone a curt nod and then turned and began walking up the slope alone.

Strat.

Strat couldn't say anything. Was there really anything he could've said. He wondered if everyone thought he was weird for just walking away. But it was too late to go back now. Strat steeled his nerves as he boldly walked forward the pathway becoming familiar he had been here once a long time ago so he knew what the village looked like but even his memory hadn't been good enough to lead his friends reliably up the mountain.

Strat was in plain sight, so he knew that he had been detected by the demons. The demons wasted no time coming after him and Strat immediately became aware of a 50-person group of demons headed his way. Their heavy footfalls making it nearly impossible for Strat not to sense them through the earth.

"Alright," Strat said to himself. "It's time to get started."

Strat drew upon the light and created a simple unadorned longsword from light. As soon as the platoon of demons saw him the didn't hesitate, they attacked. They must've been told to attack on sight," Strat mused as he stepped forward and swung his sword horizontally. It was a simple swing with minimal effort behind it, but Strat willed a wave of light to follow the path of his sword and slash outward. The wave of light grew in width quickly covering the size of the entire platoon. The wave of light ripped through the ranks of demons cutting down every single one. Strat knew he had to do it, but it still felt... well unfair when he used his full power like this. It was one of the reasons he didn't like to put his abilities on display. As Strat walked past bodies of the dissipating demons, he felt a sadness, but he continued on.

It wasn't long before another group of demons came across him. This one didn't attack him at first sight, which confused him a little bit, but he decided to just watch them. A bigger demon stepped out if front of the group of demons. This demon was over nine feet tall and unlike the other demons this one had a pair of demon wings on its back. The wings at least thirty feet in length. Having wings on the back was a sign of a high ranked demon. Unlike other demons this one had intelligence.

"Hmm a high rank, What's your name demon?" Strat asked. He was in no mood to get into a long fight, if he could get them to surrender or better yet not fight it would be ideal. The demon seemed to be in no mood for a conversation because he simply ordered one command.

"Kill the Destroyer!" The demon roared as it brandished it's black great sword and charged toward Stratos.

Strat sighed as he inwardly cringed, "The Destroyer really?" He asked. "That's what you guys are calling me." As the Demons charged toward him Stratos reached out to the nature and earth around him. Taking a step forward the earth ruptured in front of the demon's advance causing most of them to lose their footing and fall, right onto the thick roots that had just emerged from the ground. These roots took the form of giant spears as they exploded from the ground impaling the demons on them. Strat raised his sword and after a flash of light it changed form. It became a five-foot-long bow staff made with intricate designs. Strat willed fire and lightning to appear on either end of the staff. Strat twirled his weapon as he rushed to meet the demons who numbered roughly a hundred. Strat blocked the lead demon's attack and then letting the blade slide off his staff to the right Strat stepped past him. Twirling it around he stabbed the end of the staff that was caught on fire into the back of the demon. Strat will the fire to extend and a red-hot blade of fire pierced through the demon's chest. Strat heard a sizzling sound and the burnt smell of leather as the demon died. The demon doubled over it's eyes dimming. Stratos dodged a demon's spear by jumping backward on the back of the dying demon.

Twirling his staff once more Strat jumped forward over the demon who had just tried to attack him. He brought the staff down lightning end down into the ground. Lightning discharged into the ground and spread out in every direction jumping in and out of the earth, like a fish in water. Every demon within the group was hit by this wave of lightning. Within seconds the entire small army had been eradicated. Strat stood up and looked out at the carnage that he had caused. He never particularly loved this part of his job, but he couldn't argue its necessity.

"Time to go!" Stratos said to himself.

Strat wasted no time, and in only about fifteen minutes he arrived at the outskirts of a run-down village. This village had once been prosperous but after years of people fighting over the portal the village had been destroyed and the town was never rebuilt. As Strat entered the town, he became aware of just a single figure standing in the middle of town. Behind this figure was oval shaped frame. The frame was made of silver and had intricate designs etched into it. In the empty space of the frame seemed to be empty air but if Strat focused, he could see the air warping and blurring occasionally. This was a clear sign that the portal was on but not active. And there was a simple reason for that. Only a member of the Academies could activate the portal. This was the reason why the man standing in front of the portal instead of going straight into it.

As Strat entered the village, he took note of the fact that the destroyed building were aligned in a circle surrounding the portal. And that the entire village was empty except for the man standing in front of the portal. Strat approached the man. Of course, Strat knew who this man was, and a second later the man broke out into a smile.

He raised both hands toward Strat in an open gesture as if to welcome him. Once again Seth sighed, it was time for the long awaited confrontation.

Chapter 23: Clash

Strat walked up to Zach in a relaxed manor not showing any hostility. Strat was hoping he would get the chance to talk to him before they fought. While he walked Strat's eyes continuously scanned the perimeter of the village. Not for enemies but his friends. He hoped to see them sneaking around the outskirts toward the back side of the portal. Ready to make a move when Strat started "distracting" Warstroff. Unfortunately he couldn't see them. That meant that they were hidden that well, or that they hadn't entered the village yet. Either way Strat just had to hope that when the time came that they would be ready.

"Well, Stratos you certainly made quite the entrance. Tell me was it God's will that made you slaughter my troops." Strat remained calm not rising to the obvious bait that Zach was setting.

"It was God's will that brought me here and if the slaughter of your troops bothers you so much then why did you send them into a fight that you knew they couldn't win?" Strat replied evenly.

"Let's cut the crap. You know why I'm here." Zach's mocking smile remained as he shrugged.

"Oh, I know, I also know that your friends are sneaking around this little town as we speak trying to wait till I'm distracted then they're going to rush the portal. Unfortunately..." Strat felt shocked as he confirmed once again to his sadness that the traitor was among his friends that he had shared so many life and death experiences with. But, then again Zach used to be that close with him as well and he didn't even hesitate when offered power by Reaper.

As soon as the words had left Zach's mouth on the crumbling rooftops of the houses that surrounded the portal demons seemed to step from the shadows. It was almost like the shadows came together and formed. The shadow hunter demons from before! No wonder

Strat could not sense them. Strat immediately saw the demons on top of the houses to the right open fire at a spot behind one of the houses. Strat saw a flash of light and the bolts were reflected; however, Seth's group had been exposed. Strat had no more time to waste. In a flash of light, he willed his staff to reappear and stepped forward. At the same time, he activated his elemental armor that he had shown Seth before and blue- white lightning began flickering around him, the world seemed to slow down as his senses simultaneously sharpened. Strat grunted from the strain of energy he felt. However, Zach still seemed calm.

"Whoa whoa calm down buddy, I was just..."

"Jack! Seth! Make for the portal now we don't have any more time!" Immediately Strat rushed forward completely ignoring Zach's attempts to stall him. He had no interest in talking they needed to get through that portal.

Zach smile deepened into a look of triumph as the darkness seemed to gather around him and wrap him in a cloak. Zach hardly ever took off the black and red spike armor he had been given so he simply summoned a double edged two handed greatsword make of a black steel that radiated darkness and rushed to meet Strat. Strat felt the world freeze as he and his former student charged one another. The reason why Strat was in such a hurry was because he had figured out why the dragons had left earlier instead of staying behind to help Zach fight him. It wasn't like the floating fortress was in another world. The portal was just the only means of reaching the flying fortress from the ground but if you had dragons or the ability to fly that changed things. The dragons had left probably with riders to go and obtain the air gem and the only reason they hadn't left sooner was due to the fact that the fortress lay directly above them. Normally even approaching the castle by air was almost impossible due to a forcefield of air that surrounded it. And one of the only ways around that force field was to launch from directly under it.

This meant that the dragons had an almost fifteen-minute head start on them. They could already be in the fortress by now. Strat and Zach clashed at supersonic speeds causing a wave of pure force to explode outward destroying several of the already damaged houses. They exchanged a flurry of blows. Strat ducked under Zach's sword and spun his staff to hit Zach's back. A resounding clang burst forth as Strat's staff was met by Zach's sword, But Strat wasn't done yet, he willed lightning to form on the end of his staff and blast outward hoping to catch Zach by surprise and it worked. Zach's eyes widened as the lightning struck him straight in the chest. A thunderous explosion shook the mountain side as Zach was sent flying into one of the village buildings that was bigger than the rest, Strat could only assume that this building was some kind of grand hall. However, Strat could tell that this attack had done almost no real damage. This was proven when almost immediately Zach dug himself out of the rubble and threw himself back at Strat. Strat lowered himself into a defensive stance ready to keep Zach here as long as possible.

Seth

The moment they heard Strat's yell. Seth and the others knew Strat had figured something important out its why they immediately stopped focusing on the shadow demons surrounding them and immediately took off as a group toward the portal. However, the demons weren't just going to let them go. Bolts of darkness began exploding around them as a group of demons rushed to intercept them. Let's make this fast, Seth thought to himself as he hefted Sonfang and met his first attacker.

"Team tactics!" Jack yelled as he swiftly cut down a demon in his path. Seth ran drawing upon the air as he watched Aria punch the ground. The earth erupted in sharp needle like spikes that pierced many demons. But some demons simply dodged as they charged forward their lithe bodies and quick reflexes making it easy for them to dodge shut an attack. Seth concentrated drawing the wind into his palm as he pushed forward. The wind exploded forth and sent a demon about to strike Aria flying. Seth looked up and saw at least five demons closing from all directions, diving at them with reckless abandon. Seth reached out to the light and condensed a glaive of light about nine feet long.

"Duck!" He yelled at everyone. Aria immediately crouched as Seth swiped outward with the glaive and spun like a top. The blade of the glaive slashed through each demon one after the other. When he stopped all five demons were dead at their feet, and they continued forward. Rylee and Matt ran forward together dodging attack and counter attacking. Rylee and Seth made eye contact as Seth ran by her to engage another group of demons. She gave him a slight nod. But her eyes widened a moment later.

"Look out Seth!" She yelled a look of terror on her face. Seth didn't react fast enough. He spun on his heel bringing Sonfang across his body to block any attack, but he wasn't fast enough. He felt the cold bite of a demon blade and pain exploded from his hip. Seth roared in pain and brought Sonfang down on the demon's head with all his strength quickly cutting him in two armor and all.

"Into the portal," Seth heard Jack yell as Seth reached down and touch his wound. When he pulled his hand, away blood was covering his hand. Seth felt his knees give out and he realized the wound must've been way worse than he previously thought. Seth grunted as he fell to one knee using Sonfang as a crutch to keep from falling. Suddenly Seth felt arms wrap under his and lift him to his feet. Seth looked up to see John and Mike picking him up. Grim smiles on their faces as they tried to rush him forward.

"On your feet Malcovitch!" John said holding him with one hand and firing his sawed off with the other.

"You're not going to die here young one," Mike added as he cut a Shadow hunter out of the air. Seth summoned his strength and even though pain erupted from his hip and his bones screamed in protest he stood. using his left hand to cover the wound and try to staunch the bleeding. Seth suddenly had a moment of inspiration as John and Mike helped him catch up. when they did, they were at the portal. The minute Jack laid his hand on the portal. The portal began to glow with a silvery light as a swirling mass of energy converged

at the center of the portal, spinning faster and faster until it finally

stabilized as some kind of gate just wide enough for one car to pass by

without a problem. Without hesitation everyone threw themselves

forward through the portal.

Chapter 24: The Floating Fortress of Aralu

Seth felt a wave of nausea pass through him as they passed through the portal. Seth's eyes got blurry and it became impossible to make out one object from the next. Suddenly just as fast as it came the nausea passed and his vision cleared. As soon as he could focus his eyes, he realized he was in a completely different place. The blue sky was far above and them dotted with clouds and even though Seth could immediately feel that they were in the sky he couldn't enjoy it. He could already hear the sound of dragons somewhere in the fortress. It was then that pain reminded Seth of his wound and all at once he collapsed.

"Seth!" He heard Rylee cry and he felt John and Mike prop him up against a wall. There was only one way to stop the bleeding it was something Seth had thought of right before they had entered the portal. Pressing his hand to his side Seth reached out to the power of fire and he felt his hand heat up as a response. Bit by bit he increased the heat until it became searing. If the pain in his side hadn't already been enough to almost make him pass out the heat would've definitely finished the job. He'd seen this done om so many action movies and although the movies showed that it would hurt Seth never imagined it would hurt as much as it did. Thankfully, Seth's body was mostly numb, and he quickly cauterized the wound stopping the bleeding. For a few minutes, all Seth did was sit with his back to the wall eyes closed and try to recover. But he didn't have much time. He soon became aware of a massive amount of movement in the city. Through the earth Seth could feel several building sized objects that had been in the fortress had disappeared. Seth opened his eyes and took stock of the situation. He sent out an earth pulse so he could find out the layout of the fortress. And a few minutes later he couldn't help but being shocked.

To say this fortress was gigantic would be a huge understatement. It was almost the size of a small city, several miles wide and probably holding more than one hundred acres of land. The fortress had a citadel which sat at the very center of the fortress as a huge, graceful spire. It was surrounded by three walls going from shortest to tallest and made from a flawless white stone. Seth and the others were in a courtyard within the third wall's ring. The courtyard they were in was exquisite, there was a stone pathway in the shape of a cross and lining the pathway were roses, marigolds, tulips pretty much every flower Seth could recognize and several he couldn't. In the middle of the courtyard sat a massive three stage fountain adorned with a little angel that was pouring water from a bucket endlessly. Unlit lanterns hung from posts along the pathway. on one end of the courtyard was a closed steel gate that led out into another area on the other end was another gateway that led deeper into the fortress. Although Seth was surprised about the fortresses size, he was looking for a room in particular increasing his connection to the earth Seth looked until he found what he was looking for, a room deep inside the spire that was sealed by powerful elemental energies. Seth couldn't see what was inside.

Meanwhile Seth could hear the conversation his friends were having.

"Wow this place is huge!" Aria said in awe.

"How are we going to find where the gem is kept it could be anywhere." Travis commented. Seth had almost forgot he was there due to how quiet he had been lately.

"This place reminds me of home," Matt said a wistful tone in his face as he stared up at the clear sky above. Only jack wasn't speaking like Seth he had already figured out where the gem is.

Suddenly Matt's face hardened, and he looked out toward the outer parts of the fortress. "It looks like we aren't the only ones here we have incoming!"

Seth looked out and reached out with the air and just like Strat had taught him with the earth Seth sent out a pulse of wind to detect any incoming objects. He immediately detected them. There were hundreds. Seth struggled to his feet the pain in his side very evident but after analyzing the situation he knew what the best play was for them.

Seth looked to Jack and saw that the same thoughts were going through his mind however he was hesitant, and Seth knew the reason.

"Jack..." Seth started.

"No! Seth I can't do that you are already injured." Jack exclaimed earning him the attention of the entire group. As Seth had expected Jack was already thinking the exact same thing as him. Seth smiled.

"What's going on? what are you guys talking about? Seth should you be standing right now." Mike said approaching them.

"Seth wants to stay behind and hold back the dragons so we can get the gem!" Jack said. Instantly there was a chorus of voices declining. The loudest being Rylee.

"Seth we are not leaving you here!" Rylee yelled.

"Yeah man you are already injured we aren't going to let you do this," Matt said.

"We can't just Leave you; don't you want to find your mom wasn't she supposed to be here?" Michelle said. Seth shook his head a sense of calmness washing over him.

"My mom isn't here that much is obvious, and I have no idea where she is. I... I don't know if I will see her again. However, I know she would want me to get the gem at all costs and this plan has the greatest chance of succeeding."

"But you can't just ask us to..."

"Did you guys forget I already have a gem. If I need to, I can use its power." Seth all but shouted. Seth could already hear the roars as the dragons were approaching.

"Fine then if we can't change your mind, we'll stay with you," John said. Seth blinked almost shocked. Did John just acknowledge him?

"Then who will go get the..." Seth started.

"We'll split up, we don't need everyone here to go take the gem," John continued. Jack who looked like he was in deep thought nodded to himself like he had just came to a decision.

"Alright here's the lineup. Seth, John, Aria and Michelle, Mike, and Oliver will stay here, and the rest will..."

"Wait!" Rylee called as she stepped forward. "I'd like to stay behind as well." Everyone looked at her including Seth who was trying to figure out what she was thinking.

Rylee's cheeks became rosy with embarrassment. "I mean because I am the only healer here," She said. Jack nodded at this and then after a awkward silence.

"I don't give speeches," Jack said a serious but slightly embarrassed tone in his voice. Seth chuckled along with the rest of his friends.

"Yeah, you might just want to leave that to Strat!" Michelle called.

"Wouldn't want us to be killed by your depression before the demons ever get to us," Mike added. This elicited another round of laughter from the group. Jack scratched the back of his head awkwardly.

"Let's get it done." He said and a chorus of affirmatives came from his friends. Seth drew Sonfang as the group going with Jack departed quickly going over the walls of the courtyard instead of trying to find a way through the gate.

The roars quickly got louder as the dragons were now clearly visible coming at them. John stepped forward on Seth's right and Rylee on his left. Seth stood as straight as he could watching the incoming dragons, trying his best to ignore the immense pain in his side.

It was the moment of truth.

Chapter 25: For Those We Love

Seth

As Seth watched the shadow dragons' approach, there were so many of them that a shadow was literally blocking out the Sun. Each Dragon was different from the last Some were smaller than the others. Some had dark spikes poking through the thick steel like black scales of their backs. Fire was tumbling from their maws like Molten lava. Even from this distance Seth could see the cruel look in their eyes. Seth raised his hand and reach out to the light. A set of ballistae appeared on the wall in front of them tips pointing out at the dragons. Seth waited until the dragons were in range and then he let loose. Ten ballistae fired simultaneously. Normal bolts shot from a ballista would have little to no effect on a dragon but these bolts hjn-were made from the light so they exploded on impact causing Several dragons to be knocked from the sky their roars of pain shaking the whole fortress. Seth then reached out to the power of water and from the nearby fountain thick spikes of ice over five feet in length and as thick as a baseball formed. Seth Sent them flying up into the air. he added a wave of air behind them to boost their strength. But they still had minimal effect most just shattering off scales. Seth watched as the dragons opened their maws ready to attack.

"Scatter!" Seth yelled as he began to run to the side. Seth looked behind him and saw John stomp on the ground and thick roots burst out of the ground and began wrapping a cocoon around him and Rylee. Seth saw Oliver and Mike hiding behind a wall of light. Oliver's two axes were floating in front him connected at the handle. They began rotating very fast until they blurred together making a solid circle in front of him. Seth had to save his energy, so he threw himself behind a wall just as a wave of destruction bathed his world in fire. The searing heat of the black fire was much more intense than he remembered the stone wall that Seth was hiding behind was a at least a foot thick made with bricks of stone, but in front of such heat

Seth could even feel the fire through it. The stones heated up considerably but other than that the wall held.

Seth peeked out from behind the wall. The once beautiful courtyard had been destroyed. The fountain was in ruins just spraying water aimlessly. Seth checked on his friends the cocoon that Rylee and John had taken cover in was more than half melted. But it was layered so thick that its inner layers were still untouched. Mike and Oliver of the far side of the courtyard also seemed fine. Their shield was down but they seemed to be untouched. Seth wasted no time running out of cover and reaching out to the power of lightning he cupped his hands as blue sparks of lightning started to form in them. Their attacks were having almost no effect of these monstrosities... they needed to up their game.

Seth formed a small ball of condensed lighting like a pitcher he wound up and threw it as hard as he could at the closest dragon. Since there were so many dragons in such a tiny air space They couldn't dodge or maneuver very well. They could only circle the courtyard in the air at a fairly low altitude. The ball of lightning hit a dragon right on the side of his face and a thunderous blast shook the air as the electricity began jumping from one dragon to the next until it had hit at least thirty. Roars of pain and anger filled the air as dragons who were hit by lightning began falling from the sky a black smoke rising from their bodies. However, Seth didn't have time to feel excited about his success because he immediately had to jump to the side as a fire ball made of pure black fire exploded nearby throwing Seth off his feet. He hit the ground with a grunt and managed to roll to avoid being roasted by another attack.

"Seth!" Rylee shouted. "Are you okay!?" Seth willed a shield of light into existence to stop any more incoming fire balls. Seth looked up Just as Rylee and Mike unleashed a torrent of light bolts. The dragons unleashed another torrent of fire and Seth noticed that most of the dragons had stopped circling and were now just hovering in the air surrounding them from all angles.

It was then that Seth felt an overwhelming sense of danger. It was confirmed when he saw every dragon present open its maw, fire ready to be unleashed. Time seemed to freeze as a million thoughts rushed through Seth's head. he knew he was about to die, but there didn't seem to be anything he could do. As Fire from all directions flew towards them, Seth made eye contact with each of his friends in that moment.

"It's been a pleasure," John said solemnly as he pulled vines from the ground in an attempt to guard against the incoming attack. Mike's face just seemed shocked like he still couldn't believe this was happening. Michelle seemed to just smile as she condensed water around her in a shielded dome. Oliver had a grimace on his face as he raised his axes in defense. Rylee was the last one Seth made eye contact with. Her face was serene as she seemed completely calm as if she was going to simply except her death. Seth flashed back at that moment, to his promise to Joseph more than a year ago in that tiny bathroom in the small town in Kansas. He had promised to protect Rylee. So, how could he accept this death. Seth felt a familiar energy rise within himself as all his strength was drained in an instant and

a blue light seemed burst forth from within him. The last thing Seth

saw as his consciousness was fading was a massive torrent of water

appearing around him with the force of a hurricane.

Chapter 26: The Gates of Hell

In the ruins of a village upon a certain mountain a lone figure stood among the devastation. His black and red armor were scorched in several places and he was nursing his right shoulder that had a strange burnt smell coming from it. He was fresh out of a battle with the most powerful man in Elementia and he hadn't fared well. Zach had often thought about fighting his old master, he had done so plenty of times during his training but only now did he realize that his master had been holding back until now. Stratos Bannot, that name was like a curse to him however Zach could not refute his strength. Strat had been way more powerful than he had anticipated. Fortunately, as soon as the energy fluctuation from above had risen to an unprecedented level Strat had taken off a worried look on his face. He never came back through the portal.

Suddenly in front of him darkness began to gather. It condensed quickly and a humanoid form began to take shape. The shadowy figure had no face, but his voice was deep and booming when he spoke.

"Zachery it looks like you have failed your mission." It wasn't a question; the figure was stating what he already knew. Zach immediately went down to one knee in front of the shadowy figure. the shadows rolled off this man like a dark mist and began seeping into the environment around them.

"I'm sorry My lord I couldn't stop Stratos," Zach said more than a little disgruntled. The shadowed figure just chuckled.

"I didn't expect you could. There is a reason he has been able to stay alive for so long. Me and him have fought each other countless times over the centuries and although he has never been able to beat me, he is still no push over. I highly doubt he used all his power to fight you or you wouldn't be here."

"Then why...?" Zach asked in shock.

"Because you are a very stubborn person, and much too arrogant. If we are going to defeat the Academies, I have to do things differently than I have in the past. And I need you to be by my side. This was a part of your training. You need to learn that there is always a bigger fish in the seas. Arrogance gets you killed and if you get killed then you are of no use to me." Zach stayed quiet as he pondered what the voice was telling him.

"But even though your defeat here was expected, it is still vexing. However, none of that matters now." Zach looked up at the figure.

"Why is that master?" The voice was quiet as if was savoring something.

"Because the Gates of Hell have opened."

Chapter 27: War

Seth

The first thing Seth discovered when he awoke was that he was back in his house within the Academy. The Second feeling he got was the pain behind his eyes.

"Ugh my head," Seth said slowly pulling himself into a sitting position. He knew this pain. The feeling like his head had exploded and was then pieced back together like a puzzle. Seth racked his mind to remember what had happened. And then it came to him. The dragons attacked and he had used the power of the Water gem.

"Well, I always knew you were reckless, but I thought I raised you better than that?" A voice from the corner of his room said.

Seth focused his eyes on a figure sitting in the corner. As soon as his eyes adjusted, he began to tremble as tears started to stream down his face.

"I knew it!" He exclaimed as he hopped out of bed his previous pain forgotten as rushed the figure in the corner and embraced her.

"I knew God wouldn't abandon you, Mom." Arms wrapped around his head as his mother hugged him back tears in her eyes as well.

"Of course, he wouldn't abandon me," Katie said. "But I'm more proud of you. I know it must have been hard to put recovering the air gem first instead of searching for me.

Seth was beside himself with happiness, but he could not help but ask.

"So, did Jack find you in the Aralu?" His mother shook her head.

"No, because I was never there."

"Then where?"

"They let me go. It seems the I was just a diversion so that the spy could find out where the Air gem was."

"Really?" Seth asked "But that doesn't explain why they..."

"Let me go instead of killing me?" Katie finished a wry smile on her face.

"Well, that's simple they let me go to deliver a message to the entirety of the Academies. Seth looked up at his mom a confused look on his face.

"What message?"

"It's actually more of a Declaration really." Seth's eyebrows creased in growing thought.

"But what declaration would be more important to them than killing one of their enemy's leaders," Seth pondered aloud.

Katie sighed and Seth could not help but feel as if his whole world was about to change yet again.

"War," Katie replied, "It was a Declaration of War against the Academies."

Author Note (Message for the Writing)

You never know where God is going to take you. Even when you feel as if you have lost everything. Know that you still have God. And That will NEVER Change! Trust in God and he will deliver you from wherever or what ever your situation is.

Author's Note

This Story has been a ride of epic proportions and I hope you all will stick around for the ending. This story is about having faith above all others because whether you are struggling financially or physically. Mentally or spiritually faith can help you solve all of it. Lately my mind has been bogged down with the stress of bills and whether I'm doing enough for my family. And as a person who makes only eleven dollars and hour, I know how it is to live paycheck to paycheck. But I cannot stress just how much faith has gotten me through this time. Prayer is always helpful. Even when you don't know what to pray for God does so all that matters is you try and open yourself and your heart to him. He has helped me multiple times. I was working for door dash, and we only had fifteen dollars to our name and our son needed diapers. A lady who I was delivering to incidentally heard this and instead of tipping me five dollars decided to tip me 20 which allowed me to get my son some diapers. This was right after I prayed for help regarding this matter. Gif won't always answer right away or answer the way you expect but he will answer. Thank you for reading this and I hope you enjoy this series and take away something from each of these novels.

www.ingramcontent.com/pod-product-compliance
Lightning Source LLC
Chambersburg PA
CBHW031012190726
48286CB00003BA/811